FRANK O'ROURKE

AMBUSCADE

POCKET BOOKS

New York   London   Toronto   Sydney   Tokyo

POCKET BOOKS, a division of Simon & Schuster, Inc.
1230 Avenue of the Americas, New York, N.Y. 10020

Copyright © 1959 by Frank O'Rourke
Copyright renewed © 1987 by Frank O'Rourke
Cover artwork copyright © 1988 Mort Kunstler

Published by arrangement with the author

ISBN: 0-671-63684-7

First Pocket Books printing February 1988

10 9 8 7 6 5 4 3 2 1

POCKET and colophon are trademarks of
Simon & Schuster, Inc.

Printed in the U.S.A.

AMBUSCADE

────────── One ──────────

H<small>E WAS IN THE GALLOWS SHADOW, AND MUCH TOO</small>
young to die. Also, it was June. No one should leave the
earth in June.

Pablo Lovato sat on the lumpy bed in the hotel room
and tried desperately to think. Cerebration was a heart-
rending process under the finest conditions; in his present circumstance he did well to ruminate numbly on his
fate.

"Supper!"

The door opened and the deputy served stew, tortillas,
and coffee. When Pablo Lovato finished his dispirited
meal, the deputy rolled him a cigarette and scratched the
match.

"Better than the jail, no?"

"I guess so," Lovato said. "Do they try me tomorrow?"

"Sure, at nine o'clock. You are the first man on this
year's docket, think of that. Good night, Pablo."

"Good night, Chato," Lovato mumbled.

The locked door mocked him. So much had occurred
in the past hour. He was asleep in his cell when the fire
started, and acrid smoke nearly strangled him before they
hustled him across the plaza to the upstairs room. Cell

7

or hotel room, both are prisons. He had no heart to examine his latest. Now, with darkness falling and his belly filled, he looked about.

Pablo Lovato had never been inside a hotel. He marveled at the store mattress, the bureau and mirror and rug. Why, there was a closet with a door. He opened the door and peered timidly inside . . . and dropped on his knees with a half-smothered cry. Someone had forgotten a battered grip and, tied to the handle, a lariat rope.

"Mother of God!" Pablo Lovato whispered.

Wild hope of seeing another June inspired him. He tiptoed to the door and listened. Small, harmless sounds filtered through the cracked panels—a chair scraping, the deputy speaking to another man. Pablo Lovato hurried to the window, raised the sash, and leaned out. The cavernous backyard was deserted; and there was a horse tied outside the barn. His mind contorted in thought. Slowly the idea formed.

Go down the rope, take the horse, and ride. His friend would hear of the escape tomorrow and meet him at Garapata Canyon. Beyond that, his mind was blind.

He tightened the loop over the bedpost and dropped the free end until the rope struck earth. He eased over the sill, grasped the rope in his strong hands, and began his descent.

"Thank the Lord!" the sheriff said fervently. "I thought we'd have to explain it to him."

They watched from the adjoining room as Pablo Lovato led the horse across the back street onto the grassy slope. He rode slowly into the night; but he was not alone. Mundo Molimo was waiting under the big cottonwood at Santa Fe Road, and Felipe Espinosa was off to the west on the ridge above the bottoms. No matter where Pablo Lovato rode, two superb trackers would follow.

"Yes," the sheriff said, leading John Norcross into the hall. "I have known stupid men but Lovato reigns supreme."

"At last?" the deputy said.

"Yes, Chato."

"What time should I give the alarm?"

"At breakfast," the sheriff said. "Bring the waiter up, make it look good, eh?"

"I will become an actor," the deputy said. "But what a clumsy fool, like a pig in a fence corner. What if he had not found the rope, Juan?"

"Simple," John Norcross said. "Eloy would go outside and toss another up. Very bad, eh, but with Lovato you don't use the brain. Good night, Chato."

"Good night, Juan," the deputy said. "Pleasant dreams, Eloy."

"Hah!"

Eloy Sanchez and John Norcross went downstairs and passed through the lobby into the plaza. They stood in the cool June night, the big man and the small, nodding to passersby, lifting their gaze beyond the courthouse on the west plaza to the faint black mountain bulks wedging upward against the stars and deep blue sky. The plaza was bubbling with people and voices and distant music that lifted, then faded, as the guitar fought the bottle sound in the saloon. The town was overflowing with carnival spirit, for district court convened tomorrow, the once-a-year circus in which every performer was known and every act long since weighed and judged. Tomorrow began the stream of cases representing one year's trouble and strife—who owned an acre of vega land, or a sliver, who must build a line fence, who cheated the grandmother of her hoarded silver dollars, who struck first with the bottle, who must pay the legal fees from last year's session in a case already decided . . . and who was guilty of murder!

"Well," the sheriff said heavily, "for better or worse, it has begun—ah, good evening, ma'am, Mr. McGregor."

"Eloy," Bruce McGregor replied. "How are you, John?"

"Very well," Norcross said "Evening, ma'am."

The sheriff cupped his hat against his chest like a shield, watching the tiny woman and her hulking husband continue their promenade. Norcross replaced his hat on his coarse black hair, his bony face unmoved, but the strange thread-joined closeness of two lonely people lingered on like music echo. Having no logical reason, the sheriff sensed something between Norcross and Judith McGregor. They had exchanged no more than fifty words since her coming five years ago, but still the feeling persisted. Perhaps their size created an alchemy. Norcross was a small man, and she was scarcely five feet tall, no woman for the sheriff's Junoesque tastes, nor did he feel ecstasies at sight of her dark red hair. But Norcross must see more in that calm face than freckles and huge green eyes.

"A fine woman," the sheriff said cautiously.

"Yes."

Others passed and spoke. Cory Aberdeen waved, en route from his livery barn to the nightly poker game. Moments later Sal Jaramillo stepped from the dining room and spoke gravely.

"Busy night, eh."

"For you," the sheriff smiled. "One of your customers is waiting."

"Cory?"

"Yes."

"A tough player," Jaramillo chuckled. "Better not keep him waiting."

The sheriff watched Jaramillo with benevolent understanding. Sal was not the typical professional gambler. Tall and heavy-boned, wearing the same clothes without fail, he had created his own distinctive trademark. He wore dark gray Sears & Roebuck suits, open-necked brown shirts, a 3X Stetson, and one final mark of individuality—heavy black walking boots shined like mirrors. His pockets bulged with tobacco sacks, papers, cigars, matches, a deck of cards and pair of dice, pencil, notebook, and in his breast pocket the book of Hoyle. Everyone said if you needed something, just turn Sal over and shake well. He lived out of one Gladstone grip and a canvas warbag, and hotels were his only home. No one knew his origins but he had worked the river from El Paso to Rio Arriba for at least ten years. His reputation for honesty was spotless in a private game, but when he dealt for the house he obeyed house rules and such conniving was not held against him. Then too, he had other odd habits. He was always willing to help plow a garden, cut wood, drive a team. He loved to hunt in the fall and bring meat to people. "Exercise," he explained. "Man needs it in my job." His face was weather-wrinkled, he could pass for a prosperous rancher, but those clear gray eyes were the giveaway. He had the uncanny vision of the true gambler that burned bright in lampshine or midday sun. You looked at him just once and knew his tie with any piece of earth ended in his boot soles. He had no roots, he would roam through whatever allotted years he was granted, and die moving on. No matter he had stayed ten years in the river valley; tomorrow he might be gone.

He passed from view into the saloon, leaving nothing behind, and they waited for the two men who shared their worry.

"Here they come," the sheriff said.

Two men stepped from the courthouse, cigar tips rosy in the night. Blobs of shadow swimming the plaza depths,

11

they took shape in the window light as they ranged beside Norcross and the sheriff. Judge Webster was every man's picture of a district judge, fat and calm and dignified. The new district attorney from over the mountains was cat-nervous, shuffling his long legs, fingering his ascetic face, fighting an inward battle with compromises never explained in the law books. George Runnells had resisted Norcross bitterly; even now he shrank from such flaunting of the law.

"Well—?" he asked.

"On the way," Norcross said.

"You sure they won't lose him?"

"Who knows?"

Runnells choked in frustration and Judge Webster laughed soothingly. "Good enough. We'll change the venue in the morning. Anything else, John?"

"Not now."

"Then keep us posted. Come on, George."

"I don't like it. . . ." Runnells was still fretting as the judge led him into the hotel.

"Well," the sheriff said, resuming his original speech, "it has begun."

"Want a drink?"

"No, Juan. I better go around and make sure the rope hangs."

"Kick up some tracks too," Norcross said. "I'll be in my place."

The sheriff watched Norcross walk the ten steps to his office beside the hotel. John Norcross was five feet, four inches tall—at a distance, an ugly, overbalanced figure of a man with his massive shoulders and thick arms v-ing downward into his spindly legs and tiny feet. But close up he became a different man.

Some men withered when you neared them. John Norcross grew. His bony face was homely strong and marvelously expressive on occasion. He matched that face to

the separate levels of his speech, becoming bland and
agreeably forceful when he used the fluent, precise legal
phrases necessary in business; and then again, that same
face was tongue-tied before a woman like Mrs. McGregor. Children liked him instinctively, men respected him,
and women? . . . No matter his shyness, it would be
strange if they saw nothing in such a man. Everyone was
familiar with his thirty-nine years of life—growing up on
his father's small place in Moreno Valley, working out to
save money and send his younger sister through teacher's
college; and once she was teaching, he worked in Raton
and studied law with Judge Webster until he got the big
job with Jim Billings's Bar B and took over the Bar B
office in Rio Arriba. The jealous failures, of which there
was always a bumper crop, maintained that Norcross
owed his success to his sister marrying young Bob Billings. That was false. He was a big man in every way,
with the right to show his importance, yet he was self-
effacing to the point of ghostliness in his shabby work-
worn clothes. He allowed himself one touch of color, the
red and black woven belt that showed his feeling for
brightness and laughter. Few people knew that side—his
sense of humor was caustic dry—for he rarely spent it on
those who lacked the wit to understand. A strange and
lonely man; lonelier tonight as he faced a near-impossi-
ble task.

"By God," the sheriff murmured. "You must not be
wrong, Juan!"

Norcross passed through the hall and unlocked the back
door; as the chase progressed and messages arrived by
that door, he must be ready to give instant orders. In the
night a murderer was riding free, tomorrow the town
would erupt at the news. People would say, "But why
did Pablo run . . . the Brothers take care of their own
. . . yes, the fire was lucky for him . . . and that rope

. . . but why bother, why run?'' Such an act of folly was unnatural. Pablo Lovato had done nothing so terribly serious or unusual.

He had killed a neighbor in Arroyo Seco, creating a widow and fatherless child. Because the crime occurred just two weeks ago, Lovato was spared the year-long wait before court days. He was scheduled for trial tomorrow, on opening day, and there was no reason to escape. Thus the town would judge his folly, but Norcross was not concerned with Lovato the killer. Lovato rode free because, three months ago, fifty thousand dollars was stolen from the Bar B office safe and two men died in that robbery. Lovato rode free because one man, John Norcross, had overcome all opposition to his hunch.

Norcross was general manager of the Bar B, working out of his Rio Arriba office. He had one assistant, Sam Howell, to keep the books and make up payrolls. Three months ago old Jim Billings bought a herd of young stuff from Poppa Montoya. Poppa always took his pay in cash so young Bob Billings, the ranch foreman, went to Santa Fe and brought the money up on the narrow gauge to Taos Junction and on to Rio Arriba the day before Poppa came in to close the deal. Bob got in at suppertime, they tossed the sack into the safe, and went next door to eat and talk. Bob spoke mostly of Ann and the baby before he bunked down with Sam Howell in the back bedroom.

"Stay with me," Norcross said. "Sam snores, I know for a fact."

"No," Bob said. "I better ride shotgun on that safe."

Norcross went upstairs to his hotel room, smiling at Bob's concern. Nobody knew about the money and, to his knowledge, there wasn't a safecracker within three hundred miles. When they came running for him at midnight and he raced to the office, it was too late for second guesses. Someone had blown the safe, taken the money, and shot Bob and Sam who, waking, had tried to stop the robbery. Pursuit was impossible at night . . . by the time a posse was formed the unknown had thirty minutes' start.

So it had come and gone. John Norcross lived three months of silent, inheld sadness and self-accusation that turned gradually into terrible rage. He was not alone, of course, for all the Bar B from Jim to the youngest chore boy ached to find those men. Jim Billings disrupted the state capitol, appealed to Washington, but power and money were sometimes useless. No sign was found. Then, ten days ago, Norcross returned from another fruitless trip to Santa Fe, dropped in on Eloy Sanchez, and heard the latest news: Pablo Lovato had killed his neighbor. Norcross knew of Lovato, a stupid young man with a bad temper. There was nothing mysterious about the case. It was cut and dried. Norcross did not understand until Eloy Sanchez, behind locked doors, handed him the murder weapon, a twelve-gauge Winchester '97 pumpgun. Turning the shotgun in his big, square-fingered hands, Norcross understood. It was a new shotgun . . . where did Pablo Lovato get the money to buy such a gun?

"Any other time," the sheriff said, "I would think nothing of it . . . but now?"

"What have you got from him?" Norcross asked.

"Just the story. They quarreled, Peralta grabbed his ax and Pablo fired. There is no connection in that way—but a new gun!"

"Lovato has no job?"

"No."

"Money from relatives?"

"None."

"We'll trace it," Norcross said.

That was five in the afternoon. By midnight he had

visited Bar B headquarters in Moreno Valley, talked with Jim, and was far down Cimarron Canyon with three men. Behind him, fanning out to visit every store in northern New Mexico, were other men.

As luck had it, Norcross found his buyer in the Cimarron general store that very morning. Yes, it was sold for cash to a man answering Lovato's description; but more than a shotgun . . . also new boots, pants, shirt, hat, shells, a total of $39.50 paid with two double eagles. Yes, the storekeeper had one left. When Norcross held the twenty-dollar gold piece in his hand, he felt the belief rising like blood in his throat. It was new, shining, unrubbed. He gave the storekeeper a check in exchange and had the transaction witnessed and signed. For the first time in three months, there was hope.

The fifty thousand dollars had included one thousand in new double eagles, the mint shine still on them. Poppa Montoya liked the feel of a few gold pieces with his paper money . . . so, Lovato had bought a shotgun and fancy duds five weeks ago.

Norcross wore out three horses returning to Rio Arriba the same day. He met that night with the sheriff, Judge Webster, and the new district attorney just arrived to handle the June docket. Norcross explained savagely that what he proposed was a long chance, but worth taking. The sheriff gave his findings concerning Lovato's employment of the past six months. Lovato had not earned thirty-nine cents, let alone thirty-nine dollars. At that point, Runnells was all for hauling Lovato upstairs and forcing the truth. It took their combined efforts to make him realize that, *if* Lovato was implicated, his was only a minor role, and threats would mean nothing to him.

"Circumstantial evidence," Runnells said. "I don't like it."

"We'll get more tonight," Norcross said.

That night Norcross and the sheriff rode to Arroyo Seco and searched Lovato's bachelor farm. The sheriff found the new clothes hidden under the bed; and then, in the pigpen mud, they unearthed a coffee can holding eight double eagles. They reburied the can, unmolested, and returned to town. Norcross was certain now. He explained what he would do—not hoped, or intended, but what he would do.

"Let him escape!" Runnells said. "I can't allow that!"

"Listen," Norcross said coldly. "We all know the law. I say the hell with it. This is no time to split hairs. I can be wrong, God, yes, I've been wrong plenty. But I can be right, and I want to know."

"But the man is standing trial," Runnells said. "It's second-degree for sure. You just can't—"

"Oh, can't I?" Norcross said, even colder. "The judge here knows me. I'll take full responsibility, sign a paper to that effect. Do you think I want Lovato? We know him. If he was in it, he held the horses or stood outside watch, nothing more. But he knows them! Now understand me, George. I've got the judge's consent, Eloy is ready. You know Jim Billings. I want your consent and cooperation tonight, or Jim goes to the governor and your political career goes down the backhouse hole next election. . . . I hate threatening you but I am doing this my way and nothing stops me!"

"But the man's a killer," Runnells said weakly. "It is my sworn duty to prosecute."

"Is that your big worry?" Judge Webster asked.

"Well, naturally."

"Then relax," Webster said. "That part makes no difference."

"No difference!" Runnells shouted. "Judge, how can you, of all people, say that?"

"Because it won't," Webster said. "If this poor fool can lead us to those miserable, cold-blooded killers, it is worth every chance . . . dear me, I sound like a pedantic old fool but I feel exactly like a judge. As I said, it makes no difference. Take my word, you'll never convict Lovato.''

"Never convict!" Runnells said. "It's the tightest case I've ever read.''

"Oh, forget it," Webster said. "You're new over here, you'll learn. John, how do you want to do this?''

Norcross explained: Lovato had no money and a young lawyer was handling the case for experience. At the worst it was second-degree and Lovato knew he would be paroled in eighteen months at most. Therefore, even given a chance to escape, Lovato might not run from such an easy sentence. Plus the fact that he knew, very well, he would never be convicted. He must be persuaded that public opinion and past precedent were wrong . . . that he was about to be convicted and subsequently hanged in Santa Fe. Their first job was to create that fear.

"But how?" Runnells said, getting interested at last. "If all you say is true, he can't be that stupid.''

"Give us three days," the sheriff said.

"I don't understand it," Runnells muttered.

The sheriff grinned. "There are ways.''

Next morning the sheriff rode to Arroyo Seco and spoke with Lovato's mother. Swearing her to secrecy, impressing her with the seriousness of her son's position, he tolled her into town. She came to a man she could trust—Señor Norcross. She entered his office bent and fearful, gray streaks uglying her black hair, long face hollowed by grief, compressed into the wizened mould of long-suffered pain for a wayward son. She had acquired the webs and weights of age before she was old. She had no money but the sheriff knew that Señor Norcross was a good friend . . . could he help? . . .

Yes, she understood that he was not a practicing lawyer but—?

Yes, he would try. Now, if she promised to say nothing, not one word to anyone—

"Never," she said.

"Not to the Brothers either?"

"I swear."

"Then trust in me," he said gently. "And now you must go to your son."

He took her to the courthouse and the sheriff brought Lovato upstairs to a private room. She spoke with her son, fear claiming him at last through the intensity of her fear, until it multiplied in his thick mind. She repeated all the rumors the sheriff had planted and Norcross had fertilized. Then she went away and Norcross spoke with Lovato.

"I will arrange for an older lawyer," he said.

"Thank you," Lovato said, "but my mother is foolish, señor. It is not that bad."

"I must be truthful," Norcross said solemnly. "Prepare for the worst, Pablo."

"The worst—what do you mean?"

"The rope!"

"But he had the ax!"

"Listen, Pablo," Norcross said. "He was older, you could have run."

"No!"

"Oh yes," Norcross said patiently, implacably, placing one hand on Lovato's shoulder, talking on, beating him down, turning his hopes to pulp.

"But the Brothers—?"

"Cannot help you this time," Norcross said. "The new district attorney is young and eager, he must make a big name for himself, and you are his first chance. As sure as I am your friend, he will hang you!"

"But I do not deserve—"

19

"Be brave," Norcross said. "I will visit you again."

And he did, bringing darker tidings each day. The sheriff kept Lovato in a back cell and allowed no one to see him but Norcross. As the days passed Norcross communicated with Jim Billings and readied the picked men. Only those men, the sheriff and Chato Morales, and Norcross himself knew the final plan. Judge Webster said, "Don't tell us, that way we can plead innocence to a certain degree." Working against time, Norcross and the sheriff discarded a dozen ideas before Eloy struck the proper note—a false fire in the jail, oily rags placed in barrels, a general alarm, movement of prisoners into the hotel for safekeeping. The upstairs back room, the lariat rope in the closet, the horse tied below—shown those aids, even Lovato must take the bait.

"And then?" the sheriff said that final day.

"We trail him and hope," Norcross said. "If he was in it, he'll go to them for help, or they'll find him."

"Can we be sure they live here, Juan?"

"I am sure that one does not," Norcross said. "The safecracker. That was a professional job. He packed the door and blew it off with nitro, just a thud of sound. You know that. . . . But the others are here. They must be, Eloy. First, who knew the money was due that day, that Poppa Montoya was coming in next day? Jim Billings, Bob, Sam Howell, myself. Stash Perrovich and Gus Slovak went to Santa Fe with Bob and came up with him. They rode home that night. They knew. Poppa Montoya knew it. Jim saw him, and Poppa swears he told no one but his son Ernesto. Those men are above suspicion. If they told, it was a slip of the tongue. Which is exactly how it got out. Jim went over the entire deal with me. Two weeks before the money came up, he closed the deal with Poppa. Just them in the Questa saloon. They fixed the date for signing paper and payment. See what had to happen in a space of no more than twelve days? Someone found out about the money, knew where we'd keep it overnight, knew the train and stage schedules. Someone sent word to an expert safecracker, made his plans, and carried them out."

"But they did not plan on Bob and Sam."

"I doubt that they did," Norcross said. "Oh, they were set for any interference, knowing Sam slept in the back room. But they knew Sam was half-deaf and a heavy sleeper. I live in the hotel and it was odds that Bob would either go on home or bunk with me. You know how they came in—my office window on the east side, across the hall into Sam's office. Blankets on the windows, one stood guard while the expert did the work. In their socks, moving silent. When the door blew, that woke Bob. He punched Sam and they came up the hall. That's where we found them, heading for the office. . . . Someone in this town, Eloy. One, two, maybe more. I want them!"

"Juan, will they take the bait?"

"They've got to," Norcross said. "The way I see it, Lovato held the horses, helped out in other ways before and after the robbery. They paid him off in double eagles and you know damn well warned him not to spend that money for a long time. But he couldn't stand prosperity and they know that now. Come morning they'll hear he escaped, hear about the rope, guess at the horse. How or why, they won't know, but one thing is sure—he's scared, running, and a scared man will talk. So they have got to help him, get him clean out of this country."

"All possible," the sheriff said, "but when they see him?"

"They'll guess," Norcross said. "Was it luck, friends, fate? Hell no, once he talks they'll know he was practi-

cally booted out by the law, and then they'll know why.
Fine, that's what I want. I'll take it from there. I intend
to get them!"

"We," the sheriff corrected mildly.

"Yes," he said wearily. "Excuse me, Eloy."

So it was talked out, now begun, and Norcross sat
in his back room, projecting himself uselessly into the
night, fighting it before he heard the first news; tired
and unhappy and filled with rage, in what should have
been a year chock full of happy living. Nineteen
hundred and twelve—New Mexico's first year as a full-
fledged state, in a humdinger of a national election.
Wilson against Taft, with old Teddy ready to charge
back into the fray. Jim Billings was an ardent Roosevelt
man; Norcross was drawn to Teddy by sentiment, to
Wilson by cold logic, to Taft because he admired the
fat man. But it was not only the election, the sense of
participating in more than local and state affairs . . .
this was his first year of feeling that, at last, he understood a little about life and himself. That was worth a
great deal to any man. If it came earlier to some, which
was no doubt the case, he did not envy the early birds.
He had started on a horse, he might well have ended
on a horse up a side canyon ranch, but he had taken
what he had inside and whipped it over all the hills to
where he stood now . . . just a bump in the road to
some men, true, but to him it represented thirty-nine
years of learning how to live with himself.

And that was only half the battle. Now he was solving
a deeper riddle—how to live with others. He had worked
so hard, so long, he could never slow down. On Satur-
days he went at play as he worked, and it was always just
off-key to him, like turning milk or bad bacon. But
he was getting the hang of it at last. And women? All he
knew of them was tamped into a few stray nights. He
possessed nothing valuable there, not even memories.

That was his blind spot and he knew it all too well. When his sister prodded him toward the girls at dances and socials, he refused to be stampeded. If there was a woman he trusted in his own mind and heart and instinct, surely he would know her when she came. He accepted no advice on that subject. It simply could not come from others. A man went that road alone and, thinking back, Norcross felt luckier than those who jumped the fence and found themselves wrong. Better to have loved and lost, they said. What unadulterated slop! Better to wait . . . and now, when he was finding himself, just when the empty side of his life showed signs of filling, he must turn away.

But he felt no regret. Nor did he need the explain to anyone. His sense of justice was outraged. Those men had killed coldly, with design, and he would get them. He had appointed himself for the job, and, as if explaining to some higher judge, he justified his reasons—that the town was even now forgetting two dead men, as towns must invariably do. (For towns were people—not simply wood, adobe, earth—and without this ability to forget, the overwhelming weight of all the dead of two centuries would have crushed them—people, town, all.) That even Billings had begun to accept the loss, the failure to mete out justice, being old now and half-beaten at last—not by life but by his son's death. But Norcross would never forget, or stop looking, because they had destroyed his sister's life—at least until she recovered, which she would in time. But even so, something she had found, loved, and cherished was forever gone; and because he had never found her kind of joy, he treasured her happiness fiercely. He would never forget, and the only way he could lay it down for good was to find them. Not in vengeance of the eye-for-an-eye brand. He had passed far beyond that. His anger was so fierce and fiery it sterilized itself and took away the curse. Because it was not for him, but for the others.

Yes, he was implacable in some ways. Jim Billings had always maintained he missed his calling. "What should I be?" he asked once, and out of sixty years' hard-earned knowledge, strained and purified in life, not learning, Billings laughed, "A padre . . . one of those old-timers we don't see no more. Full of fire and brimstone, so damn fair they lean over backward. But when they wanted something? Man, hell was just a mud puddle they waded to get what they wanted. That's you in some ways, John. I'd hate to have you come down on me."

"That's no blessing," he said.

"Well, it ain't no drawback."

"Yes, it is," he said. "When you know damn well it's like that inside you. A man ought to have some pity too."

"You've got pity," Billings said. "But don't you know by now there's just one brand of pity worth a damn? The kind you feel for yourself. Not being ashamed, understand, but using it right. Hell's fire, you're harder on yourself than anything or anybody. Ease up a bit, son."

That was seven years ago. He had eased up, yes, but only on others, not himself. And tonight, racing time, he knew at last how those old padres felt. When morning brought the first message, he would wade through hell to get those men.

"Juan?"

"Come in, Eloy," he said thankfully.

The sheriff slipped through the back door and closed it soundlessly. "Rope is hanging, I rooted around some. Heard from the boys yet?"

"Too early."

"Early—it's midnight, Juan."

"That late?" Norcross said. "Been stewing in my own juice, I guess."

"You ought to sleep."

"Sure," he said. "What about you, eh?"

"I tried," the sheriff said candidly. "Maria kept bothering me . . . here, have a drink."

"*Gracias*," Norcross said. "With you."

He brought glasses from the buffet and poured. They spoke together, "*Salud*," and downed the brandy. "Take Sam's bed," Norcross said. "I'll bunk here on the sofa. Mundo or Felipe, one, ought to show by six."

Two

THE OLD SOFA SPRINGS HAD SEEN BETTER NIGHTS. THEY sagged and bulged; dust devils curled disagreeably from the smooth-napped cushions whenever Norcross rolled and pitched. On his face, nose massaging one faded red rose in the endless pattern conceived and called beauty by some Grand Rapids Rembrandt, he again rode a black leather caboose bunk behind Bar B steers, rumbling from the Wagon Mound yards toward Raton Pass, Trinidad, La Junta, on to Kansas City . . . oh, how a man's body was bent at the end of that trail.

"Sidetrack her," Norcross mumbled, and sat bolt upright in pearly dawn. The sheriff and Felipe Espinosa stopped poking as he came coldly, expectantly awake. "Yes?"

"Into his hole," Felipe said happily. "I am ashamed to be so late."

"So late!" the sheriff said. "This poor weakling has not slept, ridden fifty miles, wakes us at six, and he is late!"

"Oh, indeed," Norcross smiled. "But first a drink for you, Felipe, while you tell it."

"*Gracias,*" Felipe said. "Your health, friends . . . well, it is like this—"

He told how Pablo Lovato fled down Taos Creek and turned northwest across the loma, urging his borrowed horse faster with each mile deposited in his safety vault. He bypassed Arroyo Hondo and quartered steadily toward the river, descending at last into Garapata Canyon just above the gorge. He turned the horse into a corral, entered a tiny cabin, and cooked—"I tell you, we suffered," Felipe groaned. "Smelling those beans and meat. He ate and then he went to sleep."

"Not scared a bit, eh?" Norcross said.

"Nada," Felipe said. "Of course, he had no idea we were there."

"How close is Mundo to him?"

"On the south side of the canyon," Felipe said. "He don't wiggle one finger, Mundo will see."

"Where is your horse?"

"Out front as you ordered," Felipe said. "As though I came on ranch business."

"Excellent," Norcross said. "Now you must eat a good breakfast, change horses, and ride north as if returning home. Stash and Gus should be waiting up the canyon. Get them and return to Mundo. We will come tonight."

"What time, Juan?"

"How far is it?"

"Twenty—no, twenty-one miles," the sheriff said. "Leave at dusk, be there at midnight."

"Look for us then," Norcross said "We will take the Questa Road and come down the canyon."

"Juan—?"

"Yes."

"Does this prove it?" Felipe said. "Is he one of them?"

"We will know tonight," Norcross said.

Felipe grinned wickedly and went up the hall to eat

his breakfast. "Well," Norcross said, "what do you think now, Eloy?"

"I think yes," the sheriff said. "But, as you say, we should know tonight. Now let us go to the hotel and receive the terrible news of my prisoner's escape . . . ah, what an occasion for the gossips!"

Sal Jaramillo slept later than daytime men, but his ears were sensitive to the sounds that bloomed under his hotel window. Customary noises did not bother him; only strange nuances, such as those rising raucously from the plaza, woke him at seven o'clock. He tipped the green shade and looked into the plaza. Someone called, "What—?" and a man answered, "He has escaped!"

"Who?"

"Lovato!"

Jaramillo looked at everything and nothing in the sun-drenched plaza. "I'll be damned," he murmured, and because he never panicked, went unhurriedly about his toilet. Ordinarily his appearance at this ungodly hour would cause talk, but not today. It was only natural he come quickly to hear the news. He shaved and dressed, checked the contents of his pockets, and joined the milling crowd in the lobby.

"What happened?" he asked the day clerk.

"Lovato escaped."

"When . . . how?"

"Last night," the clerk said. "Window—rope."

"Had help, eh?"

"You just bet he did."

"Now why in the devil would he do that?" Jaramillo laughed. "Oh, good morning, Eloy. Forming a posse?"

"Later maybe," the sheriff said.

"Call if you need me," Jaramillo said.

"Thanks, Sal," the sheriff smiled, and turned back to his deputy. "Hear anything, Chato?"

"I tell you," the deputy said. "Not one thing—!"

Jaramillo went to the dining room, ordered his breakfast, and listened to the flood of talk. Everyone agreed that Lovato was crazy, loco, or worse . . . that he had outside help . . . but why run when the Brothers would protect him?

Jaramillo left the dining room and wandered casually down Santa Fe Road to Cory Aberdeen's livery barn. The news had preceded him. Cory was working a horse in the high corral but the helpers were chattering like magpies in the cool, dark alleyway. Jaramillo greeted them as he went on through and leaned over the corral fence. He came regularly to rent a horse and take his well-known pleasure jaunts. No one bothered him unless he requested that honor. Aberdeen waved and worked on with the horse before slapping it off and coming to the fence.

"Cigar?" Jaramillo asked.

"Thanks."

Aberdeen cupped his hands to receive the match. Puffing, he said softly, "What got into that stupid bastard?"

"Gently . . . gently."

"Sure, but how come?"

"Mac down yet?"

"No."

"I'll take a little ride," Jaramillo said. "Be back at noon. Keep Mac here, we'll talk then."

"*Bueno* . . . want the sorrel?"

"A good old horse," Jaramillo smiled. "For a good old poker player."

And casually, joking with the helpers as they saddled the sorrel, he rode off toward Canyon. Cory Aberdeen, sweating more than his labors warranted beneath his blue shirt, watched the big man move away and envied those steel nerves. Ever since the news arrived he had jangled like cheap spurs on a sporting house bed.

"Take over, Pedro," he called, and went up the alleyway to his office. From the window he could mark the approach of Bruce McGregor to his place of business adjoining the barn. Waiting, Cory Aberdeen tried to emulate a man of carefree nature, slouched in his swivel chair, boots on the table, big hands nerveless in his lap. His face portrayed that role perfectly, all the long planes and loose, leathery skin folds accentuating his wide mouth and yellow teeth which, tucked against his lips, gave him a perpetual grin.

Lean and time-leached, he had once weighed one hundred and fifty pounds following a pie-eating contest, but that was twelve years ago at twenty when young men were all belly and brawn. Still notorious for his appetite, he was unable to gain one ounce above one-forty. Everyone knew the top cowhand who busted a leg six years ago and had to sell his small, hardscrabble outfit. He bought the livery barn and, using his vast knowledge of animals, had built up a steady business. Oh yes, the town knew his every secret. He smoked cheap cigars, ate huge meals, played poker, and went on a private bender every six months. He had unending garrulity and much laughter, but for it all he was a cold, reserved man. No one looked behind that business front and saw the heavy bitterness.

For time was passing and Cory Aberdeen saw, all to clearly, the last half of his life—a barn and horses. Life had become one horse after another to him. Horses, hay, barns, and horses. He hated them at last, not the horses themselves, but all they represented—his life stuck on the tines of a pitchfork, hung on a Spanish bit, never changing. Until three months ago . . . and now he waited on McGregor, thinking of Pablo Lovato.

"I will now leave my happy home," Bruce McGregor spoke to himself. "My happy home and loving wife!"

He heard the news while drinking his customary cup of morning coffee en route to his office. McGregor moved in habit ruts begun twelve years ago and dug axle-deep in the life of Rio Arriba. At forty-seven he seemed unchanged from the day he bought his first drink and introduced himself—the big man who exuded a feeling of solidity and dependability in his round face and thick, pursed lips. McGregor had, or was born with, that pensive thoughtful look which seemed to acquire gray hair and an honest moustache as extra furniture to fill out the cheek drapes and double-chin footstool. He walked like a banker should, but rarely did, and his speech was a steady flow of small talk, smaller talk, and cultivated inanities peppered over the business lingo. For he was a businessman who took good care of his work.

He had come to Rio Arriba as agent for the stage-and-freight line which connected with the railroad at Taos Junction. Soon he became local agent for the railroad and, quite logically, acquired buying commissions for several concerns in distant cities. He bought timber and surveyed leases for mills, purchased ties for the railroad, and bought cattle for a commission firm in Kansas City. Through propinquity to Cory Aberdeen, he made small-lot deals on horses, mules, and goats. He earned three thousand dollars a year on the average, four times the sum a man needed to support wife and up to six children in Rio Arriba. He lived in a good house on Pueblo Road, with a good wife who cooked good meals and kept the place so clean he could eat the proverbial meal off the linoleum. But all he was eating, he thought morosely, was crow. When he brought Judith home five years ago, it seemed he had forged the last link in a happy life.

Outwardly, he was a doting husband, praising her talents heaven-high; to Judith he slowly became an unhappy, greedy man yearning for more than he could ever win. Cory Aberdeen sensed the truth. Sal Jaramillo was possibly the only man who knew the McGregors were a mismatched couple. McGregor finally laid himself out

31

naked on the night they met to celebrate the successful robbery. Aberdeen's worry about the killing triggered him off; that and several drinks too many.

"I had a plan," McGregor said that night. "Good or bad, it was mine. I wanted a few things from life. Not much. Just my fair share and twenty more. I never backed up either. I kept at it. Money, position, respect, a wife to be proud of—I forgot love somewhere along there—but most of all, a feeling that I belonged. You know what I mean? No, you don't, so let me explain. I came into this town and worked hard, wanted to belong, and it took me twelve years to realize that if I stayed a hundred and twelve I'd never get any closer. I even found a wife but she slipped away somehow . . . surprise you, eh? I don't mean she's cheating on me, hell no, it's worse than that, she just don't care any more. Well, there I was. I had some money, but not enough. I was respected in a way. I had a certain position. It added up to nothing. I was done. I knew it, and I had to get out. You two were like me. All the years we knew each other, we wanted the same thing, and when I saw the chance and told you, we took it. And we brought it off. We never planned on killing, but why lie to ourselves? If we had to kill to do it again, all right, we'd kill."

Yes, he talked too much that night, but he had to get it out. And now, hearing the news, he was unworried. He went down the road, unlocked his rolltop desk, and acted like the old fussbudget he thought he was not, and really was, until Aberdeen lounged around the doorframe and greeted him.

"Heard the news, Mac?"

"Yes," McGregor said. "Craziest thing in years."

"Sal stopped by," Aberdeen said. "Be back at noon and wants some talk."

"In here?"

"Be best, Mac."

"Cory," McGregor said, "you're worried and there's absolutely no cause."

"Mac, I ain't so sure."

"I say no. So will Sal."

"You mean, you won't do nothin' about Lovato?"

"Did I say that?" McGregor smiled. "I simply stated there was no cause for commotion."

Aberdeen said sourly, "We never should've used him."

"Cory," McGregor said curtly, "we both have work to do. While you are working, I defy you to find one mistake. Remember, we considered exactly what took place last night. We know what to do. Think back on it, you'll see I'm right."

But assuring Aberdeen, sending him away, McGregor began picking at the ghost of his own plan, wondering after three months if there was a chink . . .

The genesis began many years ago in three men. Nothing concrete, just a vague feeling that life was cheating them, handing out the red meat to less deserving people. McGregor wanted more and, as his marriage soured, wanted out. Aberdeen wanted to kiss all horses good-by forever. Sal Jaramillo had no illusions about the finer things. He was happy in his profession but he did want to own the greentop table and the roof overhead. Mexico was roaring with the revolution, El Paso was wide open, and ten thousand would start his own place. The times brought three men together. Aberdeen had known Sal Jaramillo many years; and being business neighbors, gave his confidence to McGregor. When the chance came it was only a matter of speaking bluntly. McGregor heard the news by accident.

He had ridden over to Taos Junction with the monthly reports. Waiting in the depot while the agent telegraphed a request for cattle cars, he noted the loading date, his ear spelling out the letters as the fist tapped the key.

"Tres Piedras chute," he said idly when the agent finished. "Must be Poppa Montoya."

"Nobody else," the agent said. "Sold a trainload to Billings. Load there, haul to Albuquerque, then back to Wagon Mound on the Santa Fe. Billings drives from there."

"I can see old Poppa," McGregor chuckled. "Taking it in cash, rubbing those double eagles."

He spoke innocently, voicing the general knowledge that Poppa always took his pay in cash. The agent mentioned that young Montoya had brought the request for cars and made certain of the date because his father would meet Billings in Rio Arriba on the day of shipment. McGregor was halfway home before it struck him. He stopped at the barn, called Aberdeen into his office, and arranged a meeting with Jaramillo that same night. When they gathered behind the corral he wasted no time. Did they want to try it? Yes, they wanted nothing better. Well, he had it at last if they could show him how to rob a safe. That they could do, yes indeed. So he told what he heard, how he knew from the loading date the time of payment.

"This depends on one thing," Aberdeen said. "Can we do it in the time left?"

"Twelve days?" Jaramillo mused. "You're sure the cash will come up the day before, Mac?"

"Has to," McGregor said. "From Santa Fe on the morning train to the junction, over here by horse or stage. And it'll go straight into Norcross's safe."

"How much will it be?" Jaramillo asked.

"I've been figuring," McGregor said. "Off the car order and present prices, it has to be around fifty thousand."

"Three-way split?"

"Yes," McGregor said.

Cory Aberdeen whispered, "Lord yes!"

"Minus expenses," Jaramillo said. "They'll run us a little over five thousand."

"Why?" McGregor said mildly. "Don't get me wrong, Sal. I mean, what will we need?"

"A good safe man," Jaramillo said, "and they come high. One other man, but he'll come dirt cheap."

"I understand the safecracker," McGregor said. "But why another man?"

"You'll see why," Jaramillo said. "You two have things to do, and here's what I've got to do—"

They planned it and worked against time to put that plan into effect. Jaramillo could come and go without comment; it was ordinary to see him dealing one night, then miss him for two or three weeks. Jaramillo packed his grip that same night, took the horse Aberdeen saddled, and left Rio Arriba. He rode first to Pablo Lovato's place near Arroyo Seco. He routed Lovato out, had him pack grub, and took him off in the night. No one missed Lovato or thought it odd that Jaramillo was gone.

He led Lovato south to the gorge and across the river into the wild country that bordered the railroad near Taos Junction. Lovato camped in a hidden canyon and Jaramillo rode on to Santa Fe. He left his horse in a livery barn, caught the first train at Lamy, changed at Albuquerque, and reached El Paso two-and-a-half days after the meeting. He found his man that same night; next morning Jaramillo was on the northbound train in one coach. In another rode a meek, bald-headed little man carrying a large, battered sample case. His name was Curly Jones and he was the personification of the drummer. They changed trains in Albuquerque, got off at Lamy, and rode into Santa Fe on the spurline. That evening the drummer took a hack to the depot, but vanished unnoticed and unremembered in the night. He rode north with Jaramillo to Lovato's hideout camp east of Taos Junction.

During this time Lovato had walked to the river and

found two strong horses tied exactly where Jaramillo had directed him. Now they rode by night, leading those extra horses, following the river north to Cedar Springs. They crossed and came to earth in the old cabin long forgotten in Garapata Canyon, an easy twenty miles from Rio Arriba. They had three days' grace to do a mountain of work. Curly Jones opened his sample case, changed into dark clothing, then opened a smaller case carried within the larger, and laid out his equipment. While Lovato watched, enthralled, Curly Jones cooked nitro and cleaned his tools. That night Jaramillo met Cory Aberdeen south of town and took the scale drawings and instructions prepared by McGregor. Beginning the next night, one day in advance of the money's expected arrival, they would put their plan into effect; and do so each night thereafter until the money came.

Jaramillo and Curly Jones studied the drawings and read McGregor's neat writing. McGregor had gotten the name of the safe, put down the approximate size of the door. He had sketched a map of the building with all windows, office rooms, adjacent buildings, doors, backyards. This was common knowledge to Jaramillo, but Curly Jones must know the terrain in case of emergency. "A cinch," Curly Jones laughed. "I know that type safe. Just an old sardine can." He measured out the nitro needed and supervised the packing of all tools, blankets, and sacks.

At sundown they left the cabin and rode in a careful circle that bypassed Arroyo Hondo. They approached Rio Arriba from the south, stopped in a little draw half a mile from town, and Jaramillo went forward alone. He met Aberdeen in the grassy bottom across the road from the livery barn . . . false alarm, nothing doing tonight.

They made the long ride back to Garapata, slept soundly, and spent the next day reviewing all facets of the plan. That night Jaramillo again went forward, met

Aberdeen, and grinned in triumph. Young Bob Billings and two guards had brought the money at five-thirty. The guards had eaten and gone on to the ranch, but Bob was gassing with Norcross in the hotel and probably asleep by now. Old Sam Howell was in his back room, as expected, but Sam was deaf and slept like a log to boot. McGregor was downtown, keeping an eye on Norcross and young Bob, who would undoubtedly bunk tonight with Norcross in the hotel.

They waited until midnight before tying the extra horses and riding through the bottoms to the last slope. Lovato held the horses while Jaramillo and Curly Jones padded silently on rubber-soled shoes into the darkness. They crossed the backyard, moved along the east side of the Bar B building, and found the window in Norcross's office. Curly Jones opened it and they slipped inside, feeling their way, knowing the position of all furniture from McGregor's neat sketch. They crossed the hall and entered Sam Howell's office. McGregor hadn't missed a lick; the front shade was drawn just as he'd predicted.

Jaramillo swung the hall door an inch from the casing. Standing guard, he peered through the crack down the hallway toward the back rooms where old Sam snored. Curly Jones worked silently, swiftly, sealing the window, taping up blankets, kneeling before the safe and laying out his tools. He lit a tiny lamp that cast a cone of light upon the safe door. He prepared the safe with nitro, soap, and blankets. He set the fuse, repacked every tool but one special bar in case the sprung door needed a final assist.

He looked up and nodded. Jaramillo nodded in return. Curly Jones brought his satchel over and placed it neatly against Jaramillo's right foot, open to receive the tiny lamp and tool. Then he lit the fuse and both men went down on their bellies. The explosion was a dull thud, the mark of a perfectly executed job, that bumped the big door against the covering blankets.

Curly Jones stripped off the blankets, opened the door, withdrew the money sack, and returned to Jaramillo's side in moments. He snuffed his lamp and dropped it, with the special tool, into his satchel; at that moment Jaramillo's left hand crossed over and clamped on Curly's arm like a vise.

They heard the two men coming from the rear. Sam Howell said querulously, "What's that you say, Bob?"

Jaramillo knew he could not act as originally planned, in case old Sam blundered in—just whack him on the head. Bob Billings was a different proposition. Then, ten feet down the hall, a match scratched into flame and Jaramillo saw the ready Colt in Bob's hand.

"What's that smell?" Bob Billings said.

Jaramillo shot Bob Billings in the heart, flung the door back, leaped over the falling body, pushed his snub-nosed .38 into old Sam's mouth, and shot again. It took only five seconds but Curly Jones was already through Norcross's office and out the window. Jaramillo followed him. They ran through the backyard, across the road, and took their horses from Lovato. Curly Jones handed his satchel and the money sack to Jaramillo. They rode from town, half a mile to the draw where the two fresh horses were tied. Lovato took the trail-weary mounts as Jaramillo and Curly Jones changed to the fresh horses.

"Pablo," Jaramillo said.

"I know what to do," Lovato said. "But what was—?"

"Then go," Jaramillo said. "I will see you soon."

Lovato swung away into the night. Jaramillo said, "Now we're for it, Curly," and led the way to the southeast. They skirted Talpa and entered Chiquita Canyon without pursuit; as Jaramillo predicted, chase was impossible in this country at night. They rode the high pass trail over U.S. Hill and camped at dawn on the eastern slopes of the Cristos above Mora. That night they circled Mora into the foothills and rode for Las Vegas. They camped at gray light, rode again at night, and got down on the edge of Las Vegas in thinning darkness. While Curly Jones changed into his neat drummer's clothes, Jaramillo took the money sack from the satchel and counted out five thousand dollars in bills.

"I thank you," Curly Jones said.

"You are welcome," Jaramillo chuckled.

"Now the part I regret," Curly Jones said, and helped bury the satchel, tools, and rough clothes under a rock. "Will I see you soon, Sal?"

"Four to six months," Jaramillo said. "When I open my place, Curly, you've got a choice—share or job."

"We shall see," Curly Jones said. "Well, good day to you, my friend."

"*Adios*, Curly," Jaramillo said. "Keep your derby dry."

Curly Jones entered the sleeping town, followed the route taught him, and reached the depot before sunrise. He sat primly in the gentleman's waiting room until the passenger came snorting down from the north. He boarded a coach, bought his ticket from the conductor, racked his derby hat, and settled into the cindery anonymity of travel. He changed trains in Albuquerque and was back in El Paso the next day.

Meanwhile Sal Jaramillo rode his backtrail in easy stages. He made a wide sweep around Rio Arriba to the cabin in Garapata Canyon. Lovato was waiting patiently and, sweating together, they led out the three horses Jaramillo must destroy—the one purchased in Santa Fe for Curly Jones, the two Aberdeen had spirited to him in the night. They dug three holes, killed the horses, and covered them with rocks and brush. Then Jaramillo paid Pablo Lovato ten double eagles and warned him not to spend the money for a while, and never in Rio Arriba. That night Lovato rode home and Jaramillo circled to the south and came jogging into town next morning. He turned the original horse over to the helper and paid Aberdeen the rental in the office.

"Tonight," he said.

They met behind the corral where Jaramillo handed over the wrapped packets of bills he had divided days ago. "Two hundred short of fifteen thousand each," he explained. "That splits the expenses close enough . . . now what are your plans, Mac?"

McGregor expounded his theory concerning their imminent departure. They must not leave at the same time, and certainly not before three months. Jaramillo agreed.

"I'll just wander off in about four," he said. "Cory, you can wait another month. Mac, you go last, eh?"

"Exactly how I figured it," McGregor said. "One thing more—I am not spending a cent of this money for at least a year, maybe longer."

"Me either," Aberdeen said, and Jaramillo nodded silent approval.

That was the end of it for them, that night. The weeks passed and their feeling of safety grew; and now, the noon hour come, McGregor looked up and saw them outside. He waved and they entered the office. McGregor spoke without preamble.

"Remember what we agreed on, Sal?"

"Yes."

"Well," McGregor said, "I'd say the time has come, eh?"

"Yes," Jaramillo said. "I'll take care of Pablo tonight."

"You'll need a horse," Aberdeen said.

"Please, at nine o'clock."

"You know," McGregor said then, "I just wonder—"

"Don't," Jaramillo said gently. "When a man wonders he thinks the wrong way, pretty soon he gets scared and does foolish things. There is no reason to be scared. Me, I am leaving in two weeks. If you wish to see me in the future, come to my establishment in El Paso." He grinned broadly. "I will set up the drinks and then take your money."

Three

NORCROSS SPENT THE ENTIRE DAY IN HIS OFFICE. ONCE, looking up from work that made no sense, he saw Judith McGregor framed in his window. Her head turned and, for the brief moment of her passage, she met his gaze. She nodded gravely and disappeared.

It had been thus with them nearly five years—a few polite words spoken, all meaningless, but a hundred glances that somehow, in some mysterious way, created a bond. It would go no further if they lived fifty years in Rio Arriba. She was not that kind; as for Norcross, the thought had never entered his mind. Only the oddity of the feeling, a warm and secret little pleasure, made him feel a lonely kinship and indulge in aimless ifs . . . if he had wandered into the Harvey restaurant in Albuquerque before McGregor, if he had seen her first, if she had looked at him first . . .

He ate supper in the dining room, went upstairs and changed clothes, buckled on his Colt, and left the hotel by the rear door. He took his horse from the Bar B stable and trotted down Ranchitos Road. The sheriff and Chato Morales swung in beside him as he passed the sheriff's gate. Moving into a mile-eating lope, they left the town behind.

·······Four·······

IN THE GORGE BOTTOM, SUBMERGED IN RIVER SOUND, Jaramillo was a lost speck in the night vastness. Tying his horse below the mouth of Garapata Canyon, tightening his moccasins, he began the final approach. Lovato waited a quarter mile up that canyon, confident his old friend would bring salvation in this hour of need.

"Have faith, Pablo," Jaramillo said. "I am coming."

He moved silently up the canyon into the trees that masked corral and cabin. Through the window, pungent on the wind, streamed the twined odors of coffee and piñon smoke. The coal oil lamp was lit. Lovato had drowned his fears in luxury tonight. Jaramillo reached the window and looked inside.

Lovato sat beside the fire, chin in hands, a grimy portrait of dejection. Jaramillo's lips shaped a greeting word to lift that head for a cleaner shot; in the act he heard subtle movement on the canyon wall.

He knew it all in one flash of perception. He did not hesitate. Jaramillo fired and saw Lovato slump to the floor. He ran, not through the trees in wall shadow, but down the canyon bottom. Someone whistled shrilly from the north. The echo bounced and sent a fading trill chasing the shot echo into the night. Another whistle came off the

43

south wall and, higher up the canyon, men sprang into movement.

Jaramillo raced along the dry watercourse, his gambler's mind unrolling the blueprint of that path from cabin to gorge, taking him safely over rocks and deadfalls, around house-sized boulders, across raspy gravel beds and sugar-crunching sandbars, free at last of the canyon, breaking into the blind immensity of the gorge, then beside the river on the tender grass in the fragrant shadow of juniper and piñon. He reached the horse and led it from the river up the secret goat path, over receding shelves and ledges, toward the distant east rim. An hour later he quit the gorge, mounted, and rode for town. He did not fear pursuit. He was not Lovato.

"They don't know me," he laughed, "but I know them. It has to be you, Norcross. You planned it all, eh? You let him escape, followed him, and you were waiting tonight. Well, he's still there and you are welcome to him. I respect you, Señor Norcross, but you cannot pull the answers from the dead!"

"Come in," Felipe Espinosa called.

Norcross had approached from up canyon with Stash Perrovich and Gus Slovak, the three forming a line across the bottom. They heard the shot and the sound of one man racing away, heard Felipe and Mundo come off the walls, and then silence. The sheriff was on the south rim, Chato Morales on the north. Before he entered the cabin, Norcross cupped his hands and shouted, "Mundo?"

"Here, Juan."

Molimo came from outer darkness into the frail door-light. He had descended recklessly and given chase a hundred yards, but stopped as his good judgment returned.

"No chance, eh?"

"No use tonight, Juan."

"ELOY?" Norcross called.

"HO—!"

"Come down . . . Chato, come on down."

"Coming!"

"Well," Norcross said. "Let's go in and kiss this one good-by."

"Not so, Juan," Felipe said. "Come in, come in—here is our pigeon, good as new."

They crowded into the tiny cabin where Felipe cradled Pablo Lovato's head in one arm. "See," Felipe said. "He fired through the window and—whoosh—it only dented this bonehead."

Norcross touched the bullet crease above Lovato's right ear, a three-inch slash that had drawn blood and knocked him unconscious.

"Bring him around," Norcross said.

Felipe wet his bandanna in the water bucket and bathed the wound. When the sheriff and Chato arrived, puffing like windy mules, the cabin grew too small for the combined bulk and sweat-smell.

"Dead?" the sheriff said. "No . . . what luck. Blessings on your hard head, Lovato."

"Hey," Felipe said impatiently. "Wake up!"

Pablo Lovato groaned and opened his eyes. The sight was not encouraging. He closed them tight and tried to shrink within himself.

"Now, Pablo," the sheriff said.

Lovato opened one eye, convinced himself that hell stocked nothing half as frightening as their faces, and groaned again.

"What—?"

"Can you hear me?" Norcross asked.

"Yes, señor . . . oh, my head hurts."

"Remarkable," Norcross said drily. "However, we did not shoot you."

"Eh—?"

"None of us," Norcross said. "We were watching, yes, but someone else came to the window and shot. Who wants you dead, Pablo?"

"Nobody," Lovato said instantly.

"Feel your head," Norcross said, and when Lovato winced, "You did that with a fingernail, Pablo?"

"No . . . but why?"

The time had come. Norcross knelt and faced Lovato in the lamplight. The sheriff squatted on one side, Chato on the other. Standing were the Bar B riders, whiskered and dirty, filled with rage that palpitated visibly to Lovato's eyes. It was not a scene of domestic tranquility; an imaginative man could visualize hot pincers and a branding iron in the background. Lovato had little imagination but he knew the Bar B. He shivered.

"We let you escape last night," Norcross said slowly. "We followed you. Do you know why? . . . Yes, now you understand. I see it in your eyes. Someone else came tonight, knowing you were here. You expected a friend, but he came to kill you. Why? Because you must not talk to us. And what can you tell us? You know what we want, Pablo. Tell us their names!"

Lovato remembered the gallows in Santa Fe. They had recaptured him and, in due time, he would hang, just as they had warned him. He could not believe that Jaramillo would come to kill him. Not his old friend, the man who trusted him and paid him so much money. Lovato was a bulldog with his teeth locked on a trust he would not betray. Let them hang him. He would never speak his friend's name. Then too, he could manage only one train of thought. He bit stubbornly into silence and lowered his eyes. Norcross spoke again.

"We know your thoughts, Pablo, but you will not hang. We tricked you into believing that. . . . Eloy, you tell him. He'll believe you."

"You will not hang," the sheriff said. "We tricked you. Now tell us, who were they?"

"I won't hang," Lovato said thickly.

"I swear it," the sheriff said. "By my saint, Pablo."

"I won't hang," Lovato repeated numbly. "But how—?"

"Make some coffee, Chato," the sheriff said. "This will take time to penetrate him."

Chato rummaged in the grub-box, started a pot of coffee, and tossed peach cans to Molimo, who hacked out the tops with his knife and passed them around for all to have a cooling drink and bite.

"Now," the sheriff said. "Who were they? Who robbed the safe and killed Roberto Billings and Sam Howell?"

"I know nothing," Lovato said.

"Here," Felipe said. "Have some peaches."

Lovato tilted the can. Juice runneled down his chin as he chewed and stared. He coughed.

"I know nothing," he said doggedly.

"You helped them," Norcross said. "Where are your new clothes?"

"I have no new clothes."

"Where did you earn the money to buy the clothes and shotgun in the Cimarron store?"

"I worked," Lovato said sullenly.

"My, how you worked," the sheriff said admiringly. "Forty dollars in cash, eh?"

"Yes," Lovato said, catching that sum and hanging on. "I worked."

"What of the hundred and sixty dollars in your pig-pen," the sheriff said. "You earned that too?"

"I know nothing."

The sheriff drank off his coffee and placed the tin cup on the table. He wiped his fat jowls and leaned forward, his face suffused with tenderness.

"Dear Pablo," he said softly. "I promised you would

not hang . . . I will keep *that* promise. But we know you helped rob the safe. We also know you did not kill Señor Billings and Sam Howell. You held the horses, stood guard, but no more. We do not want you for the robbery, Pablo, but we want those who robbed and murdered. You know them . . . you will tell us. No, you won't hang, but unless you tell us, Pablo Lovato, I will leave you with these men and ride away. You see Felipe Espinosa? He held Roberto Billings in his arms as a baby. You see Mundo Molimo? He held the first pony Roberto rode. You see Stash Perrovich and Gus Slovak? They taught him to rope. If they cannot restore your memory, we will give you the very best fifty-dollar funeral—" The sheriff sighed rather sadly and shook his head. "I am afraid the casket will not be open, however, for your mother to see your face. I could not be that cruel to her, Pablo. You know how men are when they become enraged."

"No," Lovato said.

"Yes," the sheriff said sternly. "Juan, shall we go outside?"

"Might as well," Norcross said. "Felipe, you and the boys can have him."

"We thank you!" Felipe cried happily.

Norcross followed the sheriff and Chato into the night. They sat against the cabin wall and Chato whispered, "You think it will work, Eloy?"

"Listen," the sheriff said.

Within the cabin someone was stoking the fire and Felipe Espinosa was talking— "What you think, Stash?"

"You're the fanciest," Stash Perrovich said. "I leave it to you, Felipe."

"Yah," Gus Slovak said. "You and Mundo. What you want us to do, hold him down?"

"Please," Felipe said. "No, just the arms. Mundo, what is your opinion. How shall we begin?"

Norcross stared into the darkness, a thin smile softening

the set anger of his face, yet a smile of no meaning beyond the moment. He would sit, unmoved, smiling, if it went beyond implied threats.

"—don't know this Lovato so much," Mundo was saying. "But say, remember that one in Vermejo?"

"Ah, the time with the branding iron."

"Yes, but we have no iron tonight."

"I can make one," Gus said.

"What about the water the China people use?" Mundo said.

"Yes," Felipe cried. "Wedge the mouth open with a little stick, let the water drip from a can above. In one night a man goes crazy, eh, or busts from the water. Very good, Mundo. That appeals to me greatly."

"But I don't know this Lovato," Mundo said. "Maybe he is a big water-drinker, maybe he feels no pain, or again might die too quick before he speaks. . . . No, Felipe, we must be careful. If he goes crazy he cannot talk straight, and if he feels too much pain, too quick, maybe his heart stops and he don't talk at all. Listen, we better shoot a cow."

"A cow," Felipe said. "Oh, you mean—?"

"Now you're talking." Stash said. "A good green hide and plenty of sun. I never saw that work. Did you, Mundo?"

"Not personally," Mundo said sadly, "but my grandfather told me of it. These summer months are best. You shoot a cow, skin it out, and put him inside. You sew up the hide to leave a little air hole. The best place, my grandfather said, was on a flat rock where the sun played all day long. It takes about three-and-a-half days for a strong man . . . say one day and a half for Lovato."

"I am for it," Felipe said.

"Stash," Gus Slovak said, "let's go find a cow."

They came stamping outside and walked directly to the corral. Norcross heard them smothering laughter in their

49

sleeves, shaking the rickety corral poles. Inside, Felipe and Mundo were arguing heatedly about the time Lovato would stay alive. When they agreed on a suitable wager and dug into their Levi's for money, Lovato capitulated.

"Amigos," he squeaked. "You would not do that to me?"

"Oh, shut up," Mundo said cheerfully. "You had your chance. Now take it like a man."

"AMIGOS!" Lovato cried. His voice climbed suddenly to the pitch of a choirboy in the year before his tenor turns to bass.

"Now see here, Lovato," Felipe Espinosa said impatiently. "You make too much noise and say nothing. First you will not talk, now you are acting badly and we are ashamed of you. What do you want, man? Tell the truth or die."

"Señor Norcross," Lovato gasped. "I will speak with him."

"I don't know," Felipe said doubtfully. "Maybe he has gone home. Go see, Mundo."

Mundo stepped outside and called back, "Not yet, Felipe."

"Señor," Lovato shrieked. "SEÑOR!"

Norcross led the procession into the cabin. He stood over Lovato, hands on his gunbelt, face hard as stone.

"Now what?" he said.

"Señor," Lovato said. "If I helped with the robbery, you will not hurt me for it?"

"We promised you," Norcross said.

"I did not know there would be killing," Lovato said. "I did not kill them."

"I'm not the padre," Norcross said coldly. "No prayers Lovato. Just speak the names!"

"Señor," Lovato said. "I will name one."

The sheriff grunted and scuffed his boots. The others closed more tightly about Lovato, but there was no threat in the action. They all understood, in that moment, that Lovato had fought his own personal battle with whatever conscience he owned. He would name one man, but no more. He had made up his mind to remain faithful to an unknown friend. Norcross knew which man would be named; it did not matter if Lovato refused to name another. The triumph was like wine. Lovato's stubborn, misplaced chivalry proved beyond doubt that one man, or more, lived in Rio Arriba. They could be found.

"Name the one," Norcross said quietly.

"I do not know his name," Lovato said. "He came here and stayed with me until that night. He brought many tools—" Lovato described the actions and equipment of the safecracker.

"A bald man, eh?" Norcross said.

"Like an egg, señor."

"How tall—which of us is his size?"

"Mundo."

"Five-eight," Molimo said.

"And his weight, Pablo?"

"Like Gus," Lovato said. "Very thick in the chest, a big nose, he spoke strangely."

"And he came from the south?"

"To my knowledge, señor."

"Who brought him from the south?"

"A man must keep faith," Lovato said. "You can kill me but I will not say the name. I have told you of the one who opened the safe. He—"

"Shot Roberto and Sam?" the sheriff said.

"Yes," Lovato said quickly.

"Humph," the sheriff snorted. "Well, Juan?"

Norcross said, "What do you think, Felipe?"

"He means it," Felipe said. "We could cut him into stew meat. He won't tell . . . but one thing puzzles me, Juan."

"What is that?"

51

"I did not know he had a friend."

"Nor does he," Norcross said quietly. "Come outside, please."

He led them into the night and they formed a half circle facing the door, watching Lovato as Norcross spoke softly.

"Stash, you and Gus keep him here until tomorrow night. Then bring him to town . . . Eloy, where can we put him?"

"Chato's," the sheriff said. "Someone can always stand guard."

"Good, and in the morning Felipe and Mundo will try to read the trail of our departed visitor. . . . Now, we three return tonight. Tomorrow Eloy will announce that we trailed Pablo Lovato. He ran, we fired, he fell into the river. It was dark, we have lost the body. He is dead."

"Excellent," the sheriff said. "Whoever came tonight will laugh at us. Why? Because he looked into this cabin and knew we had not questioned Lovato before he came. So he will think he killed Lovato and we, ashamed of our stupidity, must tell such a story to conceal our foolishness."

"John," Stash said, "you think he'll sneak back here for a look?"

"He might."

"Then we'll dig a grave," Stash said. "Hide it in the brush, but not too good, eh?"

"Do that," Norcross said. "Now we are late and there's much to do."

"Juan," Felipe said, "can you find the bald one?"

"I'll find him," Norcross said. "You and Mundo try to read those tracks. I'll find the bald head."

Jaramillo entered the livery barn where Cory Aberdeen, coming from a vacant stall, had waited out the endless night. While Aberdeen rubbed the black horse, Jaramillo washed in the tank and changed the tattered moccasins for his shiny boots. They buried the moccasins under the manure pile and turned the black horse into a corral.

"Anybody come?" Jaramillo asked.

"Nobody. . . . What happened?"

"Don't worry about Lovato."

"You sure, Sal?"

"I don't miss," Jaramillo said. "But here's the payoff—guess who helped him skip?"

"The Brothers?"

"No . . . Norcross."

"Sal, you think he—"

"Nothing," Jaramillo said. "They played a hunch and trailed Lovato. They were staked out around the cabin. It's funny, Cory, but nine out of ten times I'd a rode cross country and come down from above. Last night was the tenth time. I took the path into the gorge and went up afoot. He was in the cabin. Just when I got to the window, somebody cracked a stick and tipped me. I shot and got out. They chased me a way but that was useless and they knew it . . . but it proved they hadn't talked to him yet."

Aberdeen opened the front alleyway door a foot and peered up the road toward the plaza; it was hazy gray and silent over all the town. Aberdeen rubbed his arms nervously.

"Sal, maybe we ought to—"

"Norcross will be back there," Jaramillo said calmly. "Start playing the fool and give yourself away. Do that, Cory."

"Now, Sal."

"Then go about your business," Jaramillo laughed. "Sit in the game tonight. They can't track me over rock. It's all done."

"If you say so," Aberdeen said. "I'll tell Mac."

"You do that," Jaramillo said. "And watch him laugh. Mac knows a good deal."

He slipped from the barn and walked unhurriedly up

the road into the hotel backyard, took the stairs unseen, and came safely into his room. The bed was rumpled where he had lain in early night, having begged off his game with a bellyache. Now he undressed and opened a pint bottle of blackberry brandy. If someone came—on the off chance—they would find him sitting up with the grandfather of all bellyaches, sipping brandy and cursing that bowl of chili.

Drinking, Jaramillo lit a cigar and lay back to sort the odds. This was no different from a poker game. He was the dealer. Norcross had called a pat hand, tossed his discards, and made a draw. Now Norcross would sit hunched in mystery, study that draw, and prepare to bet. Sal Jaramillo had never advocated betting into a pat hand. But Norcross had no choice. Once he returned from Garapata and the news spread, Jaramillo would know how the little man intended to bluff it out.

"Two weeks' margin," Jaramillo decided. "I better go inside of two weeks."

McGregor heard the news on his way to work. Not only was Rio Arriba in the throes of court days, but an added fillip was causing all sorts of fireworks. In the night, it seemed, Norcross and the sheriff had tracked Pablo Lovato into the gorge. Lovato had gone crazy and refused to surrender. He ran, they shot, and poor Lovato tumbled into the river. They lost his body in the swift current, in the black of night. A reward of fifty dollars had been posted for recovery of the body; and all the loafers were heading for the river. Yes, McGregor agreed, poor Lovato was certainly mad to act so foolishly. No one wanted to harm him. Now he was dead, and worse, his body was missing—how would his soul find peace? It was very sad. McGregor went humming down Santa Fe Road, opened his office, and greeted his neighbor happily.

"A fine morning, Cory, a very fine morning, eh?"

"You hear the news?"

"Indeed I did," McGregor said. "Come in . . . close the door."

"They're covering up," Aberdeen said.

"What . . . well, I suspected something of the sort. Tell me what really happened."

He worked on his ledgers while Aberdeen talked, drawing papers from pigeonholes, laying them out for the day.

"Always depend on Sal," he said. "That ends the brushfire."

"Mac, how long do you figure on sitting tight?"

"Well," McGregor said, "I'll guess that Sal leaves in two weeks."

"Then me?"

"Why not," McGregor said. "A week or so after Sal. I figure on saying good-by in a month at most."

"Mac, you think I should go look for the body?"

"No," McGregor said. "You don't need the reward. If the sheriff had asked for a posse, yes, you could volunteer. Not this way. Norcross is a smart man. Don't underestimate him."

"He's that," Aberdeen said thinly, "but he's something else, too."

"Not a fortune-teller, I hope."

"I know him from way back," Aberdeen said. "He don't ever quit. When he wants something, he gets it."

They sat in the judge's hot little chamber off the courtroom, Norcross and Eloy Sanchez, Judge Webster and George Runnells. The news was published and Norcross was eager to start for Santa Fe, begin the search for a baldheaded man.

"No," Webster said firmly. "Not you, John."

"Got to," Norcross said.

"No, you've got to stay here."

"But who else—?"

"George," Webster said. "He can catch the downtrain at the Junction, be in Santa Fe tonight."

"Oh, certainly," Runnells said icily. "Just drop everything here—a dozen cases, weeks of work!"

"You have two eager young assistants," Webster said. "And several uninspiring cases on tap for the next week. You are going to Santa Fe on legal business, on my orders. At least, the town will think so. You'll have all the law in six states working for you the minute you enter the governor's office. Use all the men you need. Billings will stand the expense—right, John?"

"No limit," Norcross said. "And I agree with you. George is the man to go. But can he do it?" Norcross glanced slyly at the judge, waiting hopefully for Runnells's reaction.

Runnells slapped his hands down hard on the desk. He was caught up at last in the urgency of their emotions. And now, at long last, he smelled opportunity on the wind.

"I'll do it, John. This is my department. How much time have we got?"

"Six days," Norcross said flatly.

"Just for the record," Webster said, "how do you figure?"

"Somebody in this town," Norcross said, "is just getting up, or eating breakfast over there, or walking in the plaza. He's heard our fairy tale and he feels pretty good. But he's no fool and I lay odds he's not alone. Not counting Baldy, there's more than one man. If Felipe and Mundo can't track that horse, we've got to work through Baldy. We can't wait. Somebody here is feeling safe now. But wait two or three days nobody comes in with Lovato's body. Then our story won't sound so good. Somebody will get nervous and feel the need of a change. We can watch all the trails and roads but we can't stop everybody in this valley from going about their business. Not without evidence. So I say six days. It has to be done."

"I'll do it," Runnells said. "Keep a man at the Junction. I'll send the news every night."

"You'll send nothing," Norcross said. "When you get him, put him under wraps in Santa Fe, bring his signed statement here. I want no leaks coming up to somebody who can use them."

"So you think there's more than one in Rio Arriba?" Judge Webster asked.

"I say two, maybe three," Norcross said. "Laughing at me this morning . . . all right, sometimes I'm a pretty funny *pelado*."

Five

WAITING WAS A SINGULARLY LONELY BUSINESS. NOR-
cross sat in his office facing the plaza which swirled with
life during court days. Each morning brought the wagons, buggies, and horses to the hitch rails, swept the
people into the courthouse where, in unhurried fashion,
the lawyers fought their powderless battles and the judge
occupied his bench overlooking the long, dingy room in
which, Webster claimed, some freak of ventilation—or
lack—wafted all the eloquent odors generated by mouth
and body directly to his delicate nostrils. The jury moved
its twelve-headed shape in appreciation of evidence, of
plea, of witnesses who lied, cried, swore and tore until—
"Court adjourned until nine o'clock tomorrow morning"—and the people, wrung dry as towels on a March
wind line, came forth in late afternoon. The wagons and
buggies rattled away, people strolled the plaza in the
cooling night.

That was life unchanged in the years Norcross knew
its prime factor: the dark face of all men and women
commingled into one faceless face, the true image of the
upper river land. Understanding the advantages and lim-
itations of that life, Norcross had found patience and humor to survive. Like most people he dangled a good many

little packets from his center core—the trivial habits and favors and words, the miniature dislikes and loves, all the external bric-a-brac by which men judged their neighbors. Like chili strings on a house wall, the time came when such packets were excess baggage. That time for some people was birth, or marriage, or death, even court days; for Norcross the time was now. He had peeled himself to the bone and contained no other thought but the unseen progress of George Runnells, chasing a hairless ghost somewhere to the south.

He waited in loneliness, and it was innocently aggravated by friends who intruded upon the passage of time. Later, he recalled those days as series of incidents scattered like sunflower seed across the wasted hours.

In one, Felipe and Mundo came to him with empty hands.

"Nothing," Felipe said. "We followed his track to the rocks."

"He wore moccasins," Mundo said.

"He led the horse up a goat path to the rim," Felipe added. "A big man."

Mundo said, "You want us to watch the cabin?"

"No," he said. "Now you must stay in town. Step lightly, eh, and report to me each morning, at midday, and before bed."

"And keep our horses saddled?" Mundo asked.

"Yes."

"You want more men?" Felipe asked.

"I'll tell you when."

They faded gracefully into the background. He saw them on the plaza, in the dining room, the saloon, and in his office when they came quietly to report. One night they took him to Chato's house where Gus and Stash guarded Pablo Lovato. Norcross talked gently to Lovato who, bewildered by events, was also stripped bare of excess baggage. Lovato ate and sat and slept. His eyes were hollow, his face a bulto mask. He refused to answer the most innocent question by retreating into a dignity he claimed too late, for he had no dignity. He was a poor masquerader. Outside the house, Norcross said, "No luck there."

"He is sewed up," Gus said. "We could slice him to jerky and he'd just bleed to death saying 'No savvy.' "

"No matter," he said.

In truth, it did not matter. All that counted was passing time. Norcross rose, washed and dressed, ate in the dining room, walked to his office. Books and ledgers laid out, he worked. Faces appeared and he variously spoke, dealt, praised, dickered, paid, delayed, and assuaged. Business never stopped. He met fellow boarders in the upper hallway, vaguely familiar drummers, rare tourists, permanent guests like Jaramillo and the hotel owner and the bartender. He said good morning and good night. "Any news?" some asked, and he replied, "Nothing." Where was Runnells? Santa Fe, Albuquerque, El Paso?

One evening he accepted an empty seat in the poker game and played two hours, intent on his cards, face passive beneath the white Coleman light reflected from the green-tinted porcelain shade. Somewhere in the town a man, two men, saw him each day and laughed up their sleeves. He might eat with them, share a drink, talk business. He suspected no one and everyone.

The game broke and he stood at the bar with Jaramillo, eating a sandwich, drinking beer, discussing weather and crops and cattle prices. Cory Aberdeen limped in, helped himself to food and beer, and sheepishly confessed the awful truth: a horse had kicked him, not a bronc, but a damn livery stable nag from the Junction, driven tamely up by a drummer who thought Spanish bits were pieces of goat meat.

"Getting old," Aberdeen said. "Anybody want to buy a good barn and pair of spurs?"

"How much?"

"Just be careful there," Aberdeen said. "I might take it."

"All in your head," Jaramillo laughed. "Well, gentlemen—?"

"Enough for me," Norcross said. "Cory, take my seat."

"Gracias," Aberdeen said. "Maybe I'm luckier with the pasteboards."

Yes, it was all in his head as he walked the plaza, in the heart center of the sleeping town. Felipe and Mundo slipped from outer darkness, paced beside him, reported nothing.

"Have you heard from Señor Runnells?" Felipe asked.

"Nothing," he said. *"Buenas noches."*

"Buenas noches, Juan."

He slept soundly, but he had always been a good feeder and sleeper. And then, one afternoon, riding out while court was in session, he passed McGregor's house and saw her bent over a shovel beside her irrigation ditch.

She was shapeless in a cotton dress and huge sunbonnet; her bare legs were mud-splashed to the knees. The hired man was taking another vacation, would return *poco tiempo,* but the water ran today and she was trying to clear the ditch that came from the main ditch into her garden.

She had no business doing that sort of work. Norcross checked his horse, undecided, and in that moment she straightened to wipe her face and saw him. She waved timidly and turned away. Norcross reined the big horse around the house, got down, and took the shovel from her hands.

"Where's your man?" he asked.

"Sickness or something," she said mildly. "It's not that bad, Mister Norcross."

"You shouldn't be out here," he said curtly. "What's his name?"

"Ramon Cisneros," she said.

"So—"

He attacked the clogged ditch, cleaned the twenty-odd feet, sent the water running smoothly into her garden. Finished, he leaned on the shovel and admired the clean rows. Her garden was exceptional for such high ground. The best gardens flourished in the creek bottoms where the earth was black and a man could water daily. Otherwise the adobe accepted water, yawned damply, and baked brick-hard next day. But her garden was green, and around the house flowers and snowball bushes and vines broke the monotony of brown walls. He had never noticed the house before; it was odd how you passed a place every week or so and never saw it. Just a shape, adobe brown, a yard, nothing more. Now he looked open-eyed. Because houses were not adobe and wood. Houses were people . . . and this house was hers, not McGregor's.

"Good tomatoes," he said.

"Thank you," Judith McGregor said. "Do you—no, of course not."

"Have a garden?" he said. "Not now, used to. Never had much luck with tomatoes, potatoes either. You've got nice radishes and onions."

"Bruce likes radishes," she said. "I had no luck with them my first year, but I am getting better."

"How are the potatoes?" he asked.

"First they were all vine," she said. "Nothing under the ground."

"They need water," he said.

"I know—I do better now."

"The flowers are nice too," he said.

"Some of them," she laughed. "I tried transplanting mountain flowers. They just die."

"I know," he said.

He found himself walking through the garden, eating an onion, telling of his mother's garden in Moreno Valley so long ago. That was cattle country where even a milk cow was considered effete, but his mother not only kept a cow, she had a green thumb and a hatred of scurvy. He and his sister hand-dug the patch, dug the sidehill ditch from the creek, spread water over the slope land; and his mother raised corn and potatoes and beets and onions, enough to last most of a winter.

"Pumpkins?" she asked.

"No," he said. "Season was too short."

"I wish—" she said, and strangely, he understood.

"You know Mrs. Ortiz?" he asked.

"West of here."

"Right back there," he pointed. "She's the best in town with gardens. You ought to talk with her."

"Yes," she said softly. "I know I should."

He knew then. McGregor did not take kindly to his wife associating with Mexicans, that is, if the Mexicans were poor.

He leaned the shovel against her back porch—they found themselves standing in the meager shade—and saw her face beneath the heavy curved bow of the sunbonnet. Was it possible to feel something merely by looking, by instinct, like two animals tuned in some way on the same wind? It made no sense but he felt it strongly, more so after talking with her . . . but that wasn't entirely true. The silences between their words had counted most. Words were crutches at best, inanimate as hoe and shovel, used in the same way without conscious effort. They had never spoken past polite greeting until today, and now the words meant nothing, were unneeded. It was enough to see her face, to know that she did have big freckles, her eyes were green, her hair was dark, rich red. She seemed suddenly tongue-tied. They stood silent, scraping their feet on the footboard, his boots muddy wet, she rubbing mud from between her bare toes.

"Well," he said awkwardly. "Hope the ditch stays open."

"It will, and thank you again, Mister Norcross."

"Welcome, ma'am," he said. "If you have any more trouble with Ramon, let me know."

He touched his hat and rode south on Pueblo Road in the leaf-shadowed tunnel of the cottonwoods. Her face faded from his mind as the waiting and desire reclaimed him, for that was the afternoon of the sixth day, with Runnells due no later than early evening. Passing the Rooster Cantina, he saw Ramon Cisneros standing in the shade with his sickness, which was not of relative but of belly. He motioned Ramon to follow and led the way across the plaza to his office. He presented Ramon a cigar and mentioned that, in passing Señor McGregor's house, he saw the señora out digging the water ditch open. Was that not wrong, for a woman to work in the sun? It was indeed, Ramon agreed guiltily, and hotfooted up the road to mend his sagging fences. And that should take care of her—no need to think longer of something impossible.

But even at supper, his impatience a growing wildness, small mica-bright flashes of her streaked the seen-unseen panorama of the dining room. She was unhappy . . . that was it! The house, the flowers, the garden, inside where he had never sat, where she dusted, swept, mopped, cooked, made beds—no matter inside or out, she was unhappy. The house was McGregor's by title, but hers in heart. She had lived five years in Rio Arriba and did not know that Mrs. Ortiz grew bigger radishes than anyone in town. McGregor liked radishes, or so she said, but frowned on learning the art of growing tastier ones from a Mexican. Strange, he had never believed McGregor that critical of creed or color. . . .

Where was Runnells!

"Pie, Mister Norcross?"

"Not tonight."

"Awful good tonight."

"No thanks, Rosa."

He left the dining room and teetered on his boot heels beneath the portal, emulating all the men of past centuries who dug heels into the dirt and now into the splintery boards ringing the plaza. Bare feet, moccasins, clodhoppers, and lately the slant-heeled boots that had become the trademark of a country born to archless feet and powdery dust. Smoking, he watched the upper story lights wink off as the courthouse clerks finished the day's transcriptions. Behind him Felipe murmured, "He has come, Juan," and Mundo Molimo said, "With great news . . . we could tell!"

"There," Felipe said. "With the judge!"

"And the sheriff," Felipe said, "See, they come!"

Judge Webster and the sheriff came from the courthouse with George Runnells, all approaching in great, purposeful strides. Norcross waited in the doorway until they reached the walk. Runnells was bursting with excitement.

"John—!" he began.

"Come inside," Norcross said calmly. "Have a good trip up, George?"

"Out in the sun again," McGregor said. "Why don't you wear a bonnet?"

"I did," Judith said. "Most of the time."

"Most of the time!" he mimicked her. "Can't you act like a lady?"

"The ditch was clogged, Bruce."

"Damn it," McGregor said. "That's Cisneros's job."

"He forgot."

"Then fire him!"

"No," she said mildly. "He is a good man."

"Then tell me about it. I'll wake him up."

"I told you, Bruce."

"You did not!"

"At noon," she said calmly. "More coffee?"

They sat at the round oak table, hemmed in by the ugly, uncommonly heavy furniture McGregor had purchased long before their marriage. In those years McGregor had furtively studied other homes and determined exactly how his own must be: the best people ate in a dining room crowded by a three-drawer buffet, a round oak table, twin vases, Currier & Ives beaming steelily from rose-petal wallpaper, with a nine-by-twelve Persian rug sopping up the dust. McGregor had furnished his house from observation, not life, and his own life had turned as drab as the furniture that entombed him, as lifeless as the rubber plant luxuriating on the imitation Greek marble pedestal hewn from some Vermont quarry. Judith McGregor had brought the china, the silver, filled the vases with bright flowers. Those touches of life, and her own bright face, made the room livable. Not bearable; not after five years.

The dishes were cleared, coffee steamed between them, and McGregor was short-tempered as usual. Tonight he ground cigar ashes into the snowy tablecloth and blustered furiously about the clogged ditch. He was a great man for pecking at little things. One of his observations dealt with the fact that ladies should maintain perfect complexions; and Judith's appearance reflected his presumed position in the town. He remembered very well hearing her mention it was water day and Ramon was gone. He had forgotten by the time he closed the front gate. Now, by the looks of her face, she had paddled in the mud like a peon. If it wasn't the ditch, it was something else. She never raised her voice, raged or threw

66

tantrums, just went on serenely, growing more distant each day.

"Bruce," she said again. "More coffee?"

"No."

McGregor rose from the table and moved into the hallway toward the parlor. Time was smothering him tonight as he thought of the future and what he could do at last . . . get her away from here, show her what he could accomplish, and watch her change her tune. He had it in mind to broach the subject tonight, prepare the ground for the move.

"Bruce."

"What now?" he asked.

"I have something to say," she said.

"Well, say it."

"Bruce, it's foolish to go on this way."

McGregor turned and stared dumbly. In five years she had never asserted herself so boldly. As the seriousness of her words penetrated, McGregor found his voice.

"Just what do you mean?" he asked.

"I mean that I am going away."

"Oh, you are!" McGregor said. "And where are you going?"

"My sister's," she said. "At first."

"Your sister's," McGregor said. "You mean for a visit?"

"No."

"Judith," McGregor said. "Are you sick of this town?"

"No, Bruce."

"But you want to go somewhere else . . . all right, that's worth some thought."

"I have thought it all out," she said. "Your business is here. You don't want to leave."

"But you can, eh?"

"I can, Bruce."

Her face was so peaceful, but strong as iron. Nothing he could say or do would crack that reserve. She had more strength in her little finger than he could muster up from all his past. His present did not count, and he knew that too well. That came from living together five years. In the beginning she not only loved him, she respected him, and then the newness wore thin, she saw the town and McGregor in proper balance. In five years he'd lost her. He was still searching out, running with his promises, when she turned some corner and disappeared. Three meals a day, small talk, and the same bed were only illusions. He lived with a ghost that had more substance than he dared measure. And tonight, prepared to throw a bombshell in her lap, she brought him this . . . but wait, he thought, he would show her.

"All right, you can," he said. "But what if I sold out and left. We'd go away and find something new. What about that, Judith?"

"I don't know, Bruce."

"I had something to tell you tonight," McGregor said. "I *am* selling out. Will you give me a few weeks to settle my affairs?"

"That is your business," she said. "My sister is expecting me in two weeks."

"Judith," he said, "is there—?"

"No," she said. "I have always been faithful, Bruce. Surely you know that."

Fighting down anger, McGregor suddenly caught the beauty of the unexpected—let her go visit her sister . . . then, at any time, he could leave Rio Arriba without a hint of suspicion. Going down for my wife, boys, anything you want from the big city?

"Very well," McGregor said. "Two weeks from today you get on that stage and go visit your sister." He smiled then, for his smile was the best part of him when he chose to make it so. "Have a good time in Albuquerque.

I'll come down later and maybe we can pound some sense into my head, eh?''

George Runnells had changed in six short days. He had gone south insulated against the battering of the outer world by a fatty layer of youthful prejudice. At some unmarked moment during his absence, George Runnells saw himself as he came to Rio Arriba—an earnest, honest, well-intentioned fledgling lawyer who, by the grace of a political machine and his Abe Lincolnish face, was elected district attorney. He knew the answers to everything; whatever he missed was unimportant. Now he had experienced six days in which his eyes were opened and he absorbed a man's share of Norcross's savage, driving desire for justice.

He unbuttoned his dirty shirt and opened his briefcase. He tumbled papers onto the desk, grinned a dust-caked smile, and triumphantly spoke one name.

''Jaramillo!''

Norcross took the chair behind his desk. Felipe and Mundo turned in from the hall where they stood guard. Norcross answered softly, fooling no one, not the judge, nor the sheriff, and least of all himself.

''Tell it all.''

Runnells did not realize how he had changed, how he grew in stature as he talked. He had shown one habit in the courtroom that worried Judge Webster. He looked at people with an upward jerk of his head, like a bull wheeling in a corner and defying all the world. That mannerism was gone. His words came unaffected in one clear avalanche.

''I got to Santa Fe that first night. Went straight to the governor, he got them all out of bed . . .''

The telegrams had sizzled over the coppery wires in the night: Albuquerque, Denver, El Paso, Phoenix, Salt Lake, Tulsa, Kansas City, Cheyenne . . . on to Chicago,

Los Angeles, San Francisco. By midnight men were routed from warm beds in Austin, Dallas, Fort Worth, San Antonio, Billings, Butte, Ogden, Omaha . . . ten states responded to the governor's wire.

"Safecrackers are in a class by themselves," Runnells said. "Like society leaders. I found that out, listening, waiting for the answers. Well, the first wires started coming in the next morning. . . ."

Runnells discovered that safecrackers, an elite class, were well known to law enforcement officers in the country. They lived unmolested in certain cities because they followed the unwritten law of never operating professionally in the city of residence. But no holds were barred this time—the wires told of this man, that man, and finally at noon the wire came up from El Paso. A man answering that description was living in a small hotel near the bridge. His name was Percival Jones, nickname "Curly," he was bald-headed and filled the physical description. Known to be an expert safecracker, no charges pending, last enforced vacation at Leavenworth, released two years ago . . . and then, within minutes, the wire came from federal prison at Leavenworth, Kansas, with the complete record of Curly Jones, experience, habits, types of safe preferred, tools used . . .

"Nitro," Runnells said. "One of the best with it. Worked in the Montana mines, that's how come he went bald, something about the dynamite. Anyway . . ."

Armed with every legal paper, Runnells and the U. S. marshal left for El Paso. They arrived the following morning, reporting to the authorities, and went happily sleepless on the pinch. When they smashed into the dingy hotel room, Runnells took one look at the man rising from bed and knew Curly Jones filled the bill.

Not that Jones made it easy for them. It took five men, searching two hours, to find the money hidden outside the window under a length of siding Jones had prized up and replaced. They took Curly Jones to headquarters and commenced the inquisition. Despite the five thousand dollars, two hundred in new double eagles, Jones blandly refuted every accusation. Runnells saved their ace in the hole until Jones was partially softened up. Then he came forward on signal and delivered what he prayed was a coup de grace.

He told Curly Jones that Pablo Lovato was in custody, had named Jones as the man who opened the safe. Lovato was also ready to swear that Curly Jones was guilty of murder. That brought a bleak look to Curly's pale gray eyes. Runnells went on, giving Jones the promise that, if he turned state's evidence, his sentence would be eased, he would not be accused of murder.

Jones looked up at the other faces ringing his chair. He knew he was lucky. If he stayed in Texas, he'd get no promises, he'd hang with a minimum of tomfoolery.

"Well—?" Runnells said.

Curly Jones argued and denied and disproved until midnight; then he surrendered and dictated a statement telling all he knew of the robbery, naming Sal Jaramillo as the man who killed Bob Billings and Sam Howell. He denied the presence of anyone else. He swore that Jaramillo had never mentioned another name; but he admitted the job could not have been planned and executed by Jaramillo alone. At least one other man was involved. Why? The horses and maps, that was why. The sketches of the town, the Bar B offices—the work of a man who could read and write with skill. Then too, Jaramillo went forward on the edge of town and returned with extra horses. Someone had staked those horses out. But that was all he knew. Curly Jones signed the statement and shut up like an abused clam.

They took Curly Jones north on the morning train. The marshal wired ahead and deputies met them at Lamy with horses and they brought Jones into the capital on back-trails, put him in a private home—one of the trusted deputy's—so no one could get wind of the deal. Then, while more papers were filled with more facts and Curly Jones was taken over the same hurdles a dozen times, the U.S. marshal and attorney general reached certain conclusions which they listed. They felt the conclusions were true, beyond any shadow of doubt.

"First," Runnells said, "they are convinced, and so am I, that Jones did not shoot. Jaramillo unquestionably did the killing.

"Second, another man is involved, possibly two. The odds are, that man, or two men, are in Rio Arriba.

"Third, Jones does not know their identity.

"Fourth, and this may be a surprise to you. Jaramillo has a record in Texas, has served time at Huntsville. This was long ago, true, but he is well known along the border.

"Fifth, because of Jaramillo's past record which, by the way, is the reason I had to stay another day, we are convinced he did not tell Jones who the others were—are. And that's it, John."

"Thank you," Norcross said. "No one could do better, George."

"He's the man who runs the saloon game?" Runnells asked.

"Yes."

"Well, let's get him!"

"Please," Felipe Espinosa said politely. "Mundo and I will get him, eh?"

"Not yet," Norcross said.

Judge Webster, reading the papers, peered above his spectacles and nodded agreement. The sheriff merely smiled.

"Not yet?" Runnells said. "But here it is on a platter, John. We get him and he'll—"

"I know him," Norcross said. "Eloy knows him."

"But we've got to—!"

"Listen," Norcross said gently, and they saw the bitter twitch placed on his fury. "Listen, I knew there were two or three of them here. It's our tough luck to get Jaramillo."

"Why?"

"Because we know him," Norcross said. "Haul him in, fine, we've got an airtight case and he'll hang. But do you think he'll name the others? Not him. He's no Lovato or Curly Jones. Take him now and he'll laugh in our faces—we'll never get the other names."

"Juan," Felipe said, "you think we could persuade him?"

"Felipe," Norcross said, "would you speak a name in the same situation? . . . No, I know you, nothing would open your mouth. You know Jaramillo, he's got a little Apache in him, you couldn't get it with fire, water, or lead."

"Then what?" Runnells asked.

"I got more than I hoped for," Norcross said. "Jones and Jaramillo. Now it's my picnic. We'll do it my way, the only way. Keep Jones in Santa Fe."

"For how long?" Webster asked quietly.

"I don't know," Norcross said. "But I do know how this must be done. I want them alive, you understand. Every one of them. Mundo, go tonight to the ranch. Tell the patron I want a dozen men. The Doberniks, your brothers, Felipe's cousin, old Escudero. Bring them down tomorrow, camp three or four miles up Taos Canyon, then you come in for orders . . . and now, this is the way we do it!"

He explained his plan, the only possible way to root out two unknown men, and they nodded grim agreement. But as they adjourned, it was Runnells who looked at Judge Webster and said, "I see what you mean now,

Judge. Sometimes the law is not the best way. In fact, it seems a shame to waste the state's money on a trial.''

"Remember a lawyer's duty," Norcross said. "It is not just to convict, but to see justice done."

"Yes," Runnells said. "I know, John. It will be a pleasure to face them in the courtroom."

"George," Norcross said, "if this works, I will tell you something. You'll be a senator in five years."

"I didn't do it for that," Runnells said, speaking from the heart.

"I know," Norcross said. "That's why."

Six

A HIGHLY GOSSIPY NOTE HAD BEEN ADDED TO COURT days. The district attorney, of all people, vanished and reappeared with dramatic suddenness. Judge Webster gave an official explanation for his absence—Runnells was in Santa Fe on legal business. This was accepted with good-humored suspicion, but people lacking a juicy bone of contention soon dug up an old meatless bone and worried it around the yard. Why did Runnells *truly* go to Santa Fe? Ah, he was incompetent . . . his wife had run off with a whiskey drummer . . . Webster did not trust him in civil cases—and had not the past six days been a boring succession of arguments over corner stakes and fence? . . . But always, beneath the casual back-knifing, another feeling was taking root.

This feeling was first born in those sensitive souls who did not force the storyteller to elaborate on his basic tale, but took the simple words and built their own mind pictures. The best storyteller told his tale in brief and added just enough to make the listener visualize the unspoken drama. The sensitive ears heard shadows, yes, for shadows made unholy echoes. The sensitive eyes saw fragmentary chromos pass in review. Slowly those ears and eyes, and perhaps a nose or two steeped in the art of

75

human garbage, assembled factless facts and formed a picture. Norcross was in the frame, flanked by the sheriff and George Runnells, and—now they cast back on fishless waters—the presence of more Bar B men than was customary. Something was brewing, a fire was heating in the pot.

Jaramillo's reaction to the unknown, the unseen, far surpassed the less talented gossip-seekers. Living as he was atop a potential powder keg, all his sensitivities were amplified. A child cried and he looked for the father's hand; a woman held her stomach and he saw the rape; a drink was spilled and he wondered at the shaking hand and why the mind shivered over the glass. He puzzled at Runnells's absence and he watched Norcross with a sleepy-cat slyness, for Norcross was the dangerous man. He was the executioner.

The sheriff was another bed of catnip. Eloy was clever and deceptive but, like many capable men, needed a catalyst of the Norcross caliber to set him fulminating.

Jaramillo moved unhurriedly through those passive days, but each in turn touched him with a deeper feeling of instability. Like the lion on the ledge, waiting for the deer, he sensed the presence of a bigger lion on a higher ledge.

He reacted acutely to every word and sight and sound the night Runnells returned; toward the draggy end of the poker game two riders entered the saloon, ordered beer, and took a front table. He knew their faces in the way he recognized all ranch hands, but not their names or outfit. It seemed they were making an extended study of his face. They watched him steadily as he dealt and played. Then, going to bed, he saw another dusty rider sleeping in a lobby chair.

"Jose?" he said.

"Yes, Sal," the night clerk answered.

"Cattle due tomorrow?"

"Not that I heard of . . . why?"

"Heard some talk," Jaramillo said. "Saw a few boys tonight . . . like him over there."

"Oh, they're Bar B," Jose said. "You know how they come and go. One or two always in town."

"Yes," Jaramillo said. "I guess that's so."

He went upstairs, locked his door, and undressed. He stood against the door and listened to the night sounds chirping in the hallway—wind, snores, and crickets. He moved to the window, plucked the shade, and studied the plaza which resembled a square bowl of soft blue in the starlit night. A dog howled; a drunkard answered.

"Nerves," he chuckled. "Worse than a bride."

But even so, lighting the lamp, he removed the baseboard in the corner masked by the bed, lifted the random piece of flooring, and squeezed the tobacco pouch that held fifteen thousand dollars. He had set his departure time one week from tonight; but now he wished, illogically, that he had gone a week ago.

Norcross lingered over breakfast the next morning. He joked with Rosa and promised to try the apple pie at supper. He drank a fourth cup of coffee with two ranchers down from the San Cristobal country and set a date to look over their yearling stuff and make a firm bid for the Bar B. McGregor stopped for morning coffee, came over, and mentioned a bit of news: one of the big outfits in the Reserve country south of Magdalena was in the market for good heifer stock.

"Thanks," Norcross said. "I'll tell Jim."

"They want a thousand," McGregor said. "I wrote about reping for them. Might as well keep the money at home, eh?"

"Good idea," Norcross said. "Maybe we can work something out, Mac."

And then, as McGregor lingered, he saw another question in the heavy face. "Yes?" he said incuriously.

McGregor turned away, swung back, and seemed to collect his courage.

"You know Cisneros?"

"Which one?"

"Ramon," McGregor said. "He works for me."

"I know him," Norcross said. "What about him?"

"Just this," McGregor said. "I'm not trying to cause any commotion, understand, but I can handle my own help."

McGregor was transparent as glass. Obviously he had lit into poor Ramon and learned how Norcross opened the ditch and then sent Ramon up to make peace with Judith. If that was all McGregor meant, well and good, but if it was an offshoot of some personal quarrel between man and wife, some feeling touching on a third man . . . that was something else. Norcross looked up in anger and was instantly ashamed of his own guilty memories. McGregor lacked the imagination. He was simply a foolishly proud man defending his self-styled position. Norcross had no time for him.

"No offense meant," he said gently. And then, having smoothed the troubled waters, added for no reason at all, "It was a hot day, Mac."

"Oh . . . yes."

He left McGregor in a brown puzzle over those words; and the worst of it was, he had let his own secret thought slip. Along toward noon McGregor would get the insinuation and, if he was half a man, take steps to keep help for his wife. In *his* yard. Not hers. Norcross thought, but *his.* McGregor was a blind fool. He saw no flowers, no garden, no beauty that stemmed from his wife.

Norcross crossed the plaza and passed along the dark

hallway to the courtroom where morning session was going full-blast. Runnells was back in harness and Judge Webster nodded on the bench.

"—Señor Cruz," Runnells was saying.

Norcross stood in the hall, watching through the door, and saw at once how Runnells had changed. He seemed older, calmer, more mature. He spoke with less bombast to judge, jury, and silent faces cramming all the ancient, battered benches. It was good to see, that change, for it would influence the people. Runnells was no longer an outsider from beyond the mountains, another of those gringos from the llano. He had become a part—admittedly a tiny part now—of the life here, and would grow steadily in their estimation.

"—Señor Cruz," Runnells was questioning the witness. "Let's not rush into this, eh—"

So Runnells had picked up that much in a few days, the trick of ending questions with the soft, easy-going "eh?"

"—and now tell the court again, Señor Cruz. You recall seeing that corner stake driven into the ground on September 22nd, 1893—"

Webster had spotted him, was grinning from the bench. He smiled in appreciation of Runnells's efforts. They were like parents watching the maturing of a wayward child. He went from the courtroom into the fine warm light of day, thinking of the night when the Bar B would come in force.

"Juan?"

Felipe Espinosa had slipped from nowhere to stand beside him.

"Yes."

"As you ordered . . . it went well last night."

"Who took the saloon, Felipe?"

"Stash and Gus."

"And the lobby?"

79

"Me."

"That will start it," he said. "When Mundo and the boys come tonight, I'll have the orders ready. . . . By the way, how did Jaramillo take it last night?"

"A little *nervioso*, Juan."

"Jumpy, eh," Norcross said. "That's fine. Where did he show it, in the eyes?"

"No place . . . just something you could feel."

"He'll feel more," Norcross said. "Until tonight, eh?"

"*Bueno.*"

Norcross moved beneath the plaza trees where old men sat in humble age and children played a brash obligato against that human twilight.

"Hello, Juan."

"How are you, Uncle?" he said.

"Have you found them yet, Juan?"

"Not yet, Uncle," he said.

"But you will," the old man said. "You have good men to help, Juan."

Yes, he was thinking how fine it was to have such men beside him, men he could trust with his life. He opened the office and worked steadily until noon, stepped next door for dinner, and waited patiently to make his next move.

When Jaramillo entered the dining room, Norcross gave him a level stare, a brief nod, and walked away. That was his opening gesture, planned since last night, a deliberate refusal to speak. That might push Jaramillo slightly off balance, set him thinking and wondering, watching closer . . . and most of all, Jaramillo would tell other men who had watched John Norcross for months.

Now let them watch, let them begin to feel the first doubt and fear as it grew in the very marrow of Jaramillo. For Jaramillo must tell them his suspicions and it was

80

human nature for them to watch the gambler and wonder, "Will he betray us?" and then Norcross would see if they could outlast him, if they could stand the pressure of imminent death. It was so easy to give death second-hand—as they gave it to Bob and Sam—but the boot was on the other foot now, or at least their toes were just between the pull loops . . . and heading down!

Darkness cloaked the movement of many men that night. Bar B riders guarded all roads leading from Rio Arriba. They took turns watching and dozing, and no man left the town unseen. They looked particularly for one man, in case he jumped the gun, and for any man who acted suspiciously.

Bright lamplight revealed the movements of other men. An old man, bent and feeble, roosted like a moulting crow at the saloon bar. He wore patched trousers and a pullover shirt, his boots were deeply scarred, his hat an eloquent testimonial to the endurance of Stetson. It had suffered untold tortures and still resembled a hat; it was a perfect topper for the old man who, more than his hat, had triumphed over life. His name was Escudero and he was no more feeble than a healthy rattlesnake. Past seventy, he was still top rope man on the Bar B, a true artist who taught the children their first loops and gave the young men lessons in skill. To the bartender's knowledge, Escudero visited Rio Arriba once a year at most. He kept his money in a greasy coin purse and made each beer last an hour, and tonight he watched the poker game, his gaze fixed unwaveringly on the back of Jaramillo's head. Occasionally he glanced across the long, smoky room toward the two Bar B men lounging up front. Norcross had said, "Watch him, Cisco. Make him feel your anger," and old Escudero had replied, "I will crucify him, Juan." For Escudero had loved Bob Billings as a son. If Jaramillo had felt that depthless hatred pounding like waves against him, the game would long since have dissolved.

And again in darkness, behind the hotel, Felipe and Mundo waited patiently to take their positions. When Jaramillo went to bed they would guard back door and lobby; and other men watched the front and side windows.

The sheriff wandered aimlessly that night, in and out of the saloons, through the hotel, the courthouse, the cell block, back to the plaza. Chato Morales spent his time outside the general store cater-cornered from the hotel on the west plaza. No man was conspicuous. No man drew attention. But the moment neared when, as one man, their presence would loom higher than Taos Mountain. Indeed, the first tingles were felt that night.

Jaramillo cashed the chips, closed the game, and walked stiff-legged to the hotel. He saw a rider in the same rocking chair, not last night's man or this noon's, but a stranger with fresh dust on his Levi's and a ginger-colored beard dirtying his lean jaw. Cory Aberdeen chose that moment to open the front door and call, "Hey, Sal!" and the man in the rocker tilted his head back. His face took shape under the wide hat brim, eyes closed but jaw tightening. He was not asleep.

"Yes?" Jaramillo said. "What's the trouble, I short-change you?"

"Nothing, Sal. Just wondered if you wanted a horse tomorrow?"

"Maybe . . . why?"

"Because that black, he's gone lame. I got a good sorrel though."

"You know me," Jaramillo said. "Any old broomtail will do."

"*Bueno* . . . 'night, Sal."

"Good night, Cory."

Furious at Aberdeen, Jaramillo took the stairs and searched hopefully for safety in the drafty, creaky hallway. Aberdeen wanted to see him tomorrow and had tipped him in the best way—a natural question about the horse; and yet, tonight, all words and actions were suddenly suspect. Jaramillo locked his door and sat, drinking brandy, staring up at the brown wall.

"Nerves," he said, and then, "No, something's up."

One more day. He would give himself until tomorrow night to shed the jumps or prove something he did not want to know.

Aberdeen was waiting like a faithful suitor when McGregor came down the road next morning. He followed McGregor into the commission office, closed the door, and spoke his fears.

"Mac, something's wrong."

"Not again," McGregor said. "You're worse than an old maid, Cory. Lose last night?"

"I won eleven dollars," Aberdeen said righteously. "And this, by God, is not imagination!"

"Then what is it?"

"Sal was on the prod last night," Aberdeen said. "Nobody else saw it, but I did. All through the game and when I tipped him to come down this noon . . . now don't go poking fun at me, Mac."

"That's all?"

"That's plenty," Aberdeen said. "I know him better'n you ever will. If something is sideways in his craw, we've got to know."

"Well, ask him," McGregor said. "He's not a mind reader."

"That's where you're wrong," Aberdeen said. "You wait, you'll see."

McGregor slammed his pencil on the desk. "Cory, I'm

getting fed up. For the last time, what could possibly be wrong? Nothing, absolutely nothing. Just shovel your manure and stop running from ghosts.''

"No ghosts," Aberdeen said doggedly.

He had faced danger in his life, many shapes and sizes, from broncs to barroom brawls and guns. He came through that wreckage untouched, but now an alien fear was chilling him. It had no name, not even shape, but he felt that all the disconnected incidents were forming a pattern, hammering a weapon that might well rip his life away.

"No ghosts," he repeated. "No sir. You wait till Sal comes, you'll see."

Jaramillo had thrown off his womanish vapors when he came downstairs at noon and saw another rider in the lobby rocker. Once meant nothing, twice was coincidence, three times was not definite proof; but the fourth time was a shock. Entering the dining room was another dull thud against his complacency. He spoke to Norcross and received one stiff nod in passing. That was the second time Norcross failed to speak. Such conduct was unforgivable after so many years acquaintance. It was almost as if Norcross wanted deliberately to rub him the wrong way. But why? Jaramillo ate quickly and went from the hotel down Santa Fe Road to the livery barn.

"Cory?" he asked the helpers.

"Out back, Sal . . . say, the black is lame."

"I know," he said, "and that sorrel better be gentle."

"For old ladies, Sal."

"That's for me," he smiled, and heard their laughter tease him through the alleyway to the corral where Aberdeen was kicking up dust, showing off the fine points of a bronc to McGregor. Their presence was nicely planned, above suspicion, and he hated every part of the scene. He leaned on the fence until Aberdeen jerked the halter and came over with McGregor. Two inside, one out, forearms on the slick-worn topboard, three gentlemen of leisure on a hot June day. Would they kick a cripple or rob a blind man's cup? Never. But kill a man? Ah, that was something else again.

"Cigar?" Jaramillo said.

Aberdeen shifted his weight and glanced toward the alleyway. Someone could stand unseen in that mote-clogged shadow and overhear private words. The ghosts were roosting in Aberdeen's hat.

"No thanks," he said impatiently.

"Cigar?" Jaramillo murmured.

"Take it," McGregor said softly. "Smoke and grin, Cory, stand here and point at that nag and act like a human being. Sal, our friend has got the D.T.'s or a damn good facsimile . . . hold that match . . . says you're all steamed up over something?"

Looking beyond them, but into them, Jaramillo felt like the thumb in the dike. If he admitted his growing suspicion, they would panic. Oh, McGregor would deny his fallibility. Mac took great pride in his coolness under pressure, but the truth was, Mac had never suffered great pressure. Fear was worse than honey; it stuck and stretched, passed from one man to another invisibly. Aberdeen was no coward but he would run because it was the last way out. That was only natural. McGregor, on the other hand, was unpredictable. Up to some crucial moment Mac would be the sanest, clearest-thinking man in town . . . and then, if the unexpected blasted him, he might turn even cooler or blow out his own brains. Jaramillo had to walk a tightrope. He could tell them a little, but no more.

"Not steamed up," he lied. "Just a little *cuidado*, you know, worried in general."

"About what?"

"Can't put my finger on it, Mac."

"You see," Aberdeen hissed. "Sal, you think they—?"

"No," Jaramillo said. "Not a chance."

"Then why—?"

"Go saddle me a horse," Jaramillo said. "I'm taking my *pasear* in five minutes . . . go on, Cory!"

Aberdeen climbed the fence and disappeared into the barn. McGregor crawled laboriously over the topboard and stood beside Jaramillo, puffing his cigar, smiling blandly at the sky.

"Nothing you can put a finger on, Sal?"

"Just a feeling, Mac. Too many Bar B men in town."

"Business maybe?"

"No," Jaramillo said. "I think Norcross is trying one last trick."

"Put on some pressure," McGregor said understandingly. "Sure, that's an old game. Try to smoke the skunks out—no offense meant, Sal . . . but that's all?"

"That's the way I see it."

"Well then," McGregor said, "does this change your plan?"

"Not a day," Jaramillo said. "I'm leaving next week, just like I told you."

"But if you change your mind for some damn good reason," McGregor said, "you'll let us know?"

"I will, Mac."

"Or anything else, eh?"

"Listen, Mac," Jaramillo said calmly. "The only way they can get to me is through Pablo and Curly. Pablo's dead and they'll never find Curly. But let's cover all the bets. If they did find me, that's no reason for you to bolt, Mac. And remember, don't let Cory go loco. They can't get you two, and you know why."

86

"I know why," McGregor said. "It has to come from you to them, and I know you, Sal."

"Thank you," Jaramillo murmured. "My mother never spoke kinder words . . . *adios*, Mac."

The afternoon court session was droning along with the bottle flies and the dry heat when Felipe Espinosa tied his horse at the rail and entered the Bar B office.

"He got a horse," Felipe said. "From the barn. He is riding east."

"They know it there?" Norcross asked.

"Five men watch him," Felipe smiled. "But he takes a ride every day. This is nothing."

"Who was at the barn?"

"Oh, all the boys," Felipe said. "Aberdeen and Señor McGregor, but they are always around. Nothing of a suspicious nature."

"Watch him," Norcross said. "Tell Escudero to take the same seat tonight. I will play in the poker game."

"Ah," Felipe said happily. "Now we get to the meat."

"Closer," he said. "After supper then?"

"Bueno."

As Jaramillo rode away, McGregor tried to explain the lack of danger.

"Sal told me he was acting foolish."

"Sal!" Aberdeen said. "He never acted foolish in his life."

"Cory, what's on your mind?"

"Well—"

"Yes, well!" McGregor snapped. "Sal gets nervous and you want to clear out. There's a real sensible thing to do."

"But I tell you, this Norcross—"

"Damn Norcross!" McGregor said. "He's barking

at the moon. Even if he knew about Sal, how could he name us? He can't, and you know why. Lovato and Jones never saw us, much less heard our names. Sal won't tell.''

"I'm not talking about Sal," Aberdeen said. "You just don't know the Bar B. If they get hold of Sal, he'll talk . . . my God, Mac, they don't go by any law book. You can set around if you want. I'm watching Sal close and the first time he—"

"You'll make a run for it, eh?"

"Yes."

"With your end of the money?"

"Sure—" and Aberdeen looked up.

"Oh sure," McGregor said softly. "Take it and run. If they stop you, what do you say—won it in a poker game, your grandma died? That's doing exactly what Norcross wants."

"But I can't leave it," Aberdeen said. "I won't dare come back, once I pull out."

"Not if you leave in a cloud of dust," McGregor said. "Not the way Norcross is watching everybody in this town. That's why Sal is nervy. He's got a talent for feeling eyes, not only on him but on anybody around him. Norcross is playing a game, putting on pressure, and some of it is bound to rub off on Sal. Norcross is waiting for somebody to make a break . . . so go on. You want to be first?"

"You think that's it," Aberdeen said. "Honest-to-God, Mac?"

"Absolutely all," McGregor said. "Just sit tight. We'll leave here safe as angels."

"But I sure can't leave that money," Aberdeen said stubbornly. "No matter what happens."

"It's a problem," McGregor said. "I've tried to figure the best way."

"How's that, Mac?"

"Nothing," McGregor smiled. "Keep on doing what I'm expected to do. Run my business and sit tight. Now you go back to work and stop worrying."

But McGregor lied knowingly, willingly, thinking of Jaramillo and Norcross, wondering against his better judgment if there was more than met the eye.

Seven

THE LIVELY-IF-NOT-DEATHLESS HISTORY UNFOLDING IN the courtroom seemed to energize people. Merchants stayed open after supper, the hotel was jam-packed, even small boys collected nickels by guarding wagons and buggies. The ladies were stimulated in the manner of Joseph and ran up bright-hued dresses on their Singers. But these offshoots were pale wine compared to the singular conduct of men. Give a man a good trial or hanging, Judge Webster said, and he'd prove how foolish man could be.

The men gathered nightly in the saloon to drink, argue, fight, and cry, as men had done since the Year One. But in Rio Arriba, during court days, nothing equalled the wire-taut excitement of the poker game. From eight o'clock starting time until cash-in, faces changed as fortunes waned but the chairs never cooled. The poker players were dedicated men, almost fanatical, and they faced Jaramillo as knights of old squared off against the dragon. And Jaramillo, in past years, had welcomed court days. They meant higher stakes and larger profits.

But now?

He came from the hotel that evening, set out the chip

rack, seated himself, sized the stacks, adjusted his green-tinted visor, and nodded genially. "Gentlemen," he said, but his heart was not in his work. He saw those now-familiar faces, bearded, leathery, and the old man at the back bar who nursed a private anger.

A man took the last vacant chair and Jaramillo smiled. "Sorry."

"Oh—Cory?"

"Yes," Jaramillo said, "but stick around. We'll give him five minutes, eh?"

"Sure, Sal."

Jaramillo collected money for the stacks, broke the seal on a fresh deck, and fanned the cards. This moment was a tradition. He mixed the suits with careless skill, sized the deck, and executed the waterfall shuffle as a touch of theatrics.

"Draw and stud," he intoned. "Ante up, gentlemen. Good luck to you all."

He settled foursquare in his chair and dealt the first hand, cigar ashes dribbling on his shirt front, big hands moving easily as he began the game, taking the house cut so unobtrusively that, as many a man said, "You don't even feel the pain when Sal grabs the cut." For a few minutes, concentrating entirely on the game, fear was ignored. Then Cory Aberdeen took the reserved chair and made his presence felt, smoking endless cigarettes, riffling his chips, flashing his yellow-toothed grin at good plays and bad sallies . . . but now and then he craned his long neck like a nervous snipe and peered through the blue smoke fog at the jostling crowd.

The play droned on, men ringed the big table, the clock marched . . . eight-thirty, nine, climbing toward ten. Jaramillo lit his fifth cigar and wondered if it would happen, when he would know beyond the last shadow of doubt.

* * *

Gathered in the back room, they waited for orders. But first, it seemed, Escudero had sent a personal request with Felipe.

"He wants Jaramillo, Juan."

"We all want him," Norcross said. "Remind Cisco we want him alive . . . yes, he can have the honor if it breaks his way."

"He will thank you," Felipe said. "Now of tonight?"

"Take the same places," Norcross said. "At ten o'clock I'll buck the tiger."

"No empty chairs," Chato warned.

"Oh yes," Norcross smiled. "Our man is playing now."

"Who?"

"Jess Dobernik."

"And then?" the sheriff asked.

"I'll stay with Jaramillo all the way," Norcross said. "I want him to know it tonight. He's tough but I think there's a way—"

He paused and they waited silently, Judge Webster and Runnells, the sheriff and Chato Morales, Felipe and Mundo. They wondered how he would break Jaramillo, make that strong man lose nerve, force him to run . . . and then, yes, what then? This was a battle of the mind, not the simple business of chasing a frightened man over the hills.

"—and if he does," Norcross said, "he won't waste time. From tonight on we've got to be ready."

"Juan," the sheriff said, "I understand we want him to run so we can catch him with the money. But will he warn the others?"

"Yes," Norcross said. "That is the most important part. Starting tonight, we watch him every minute. Remember, to warn others he must speak to them, so we watch every man he sees."

"Eih," Chato said. "We are lucky he's not a padre, eh."

"Not so lucky," Norcross said. "He knows what we want him to do, he'll make it hard for us . . . but we want it that way. I want to tear the guts out of him. . . . Now, time to go."

He went up the hall and let himself out the front door where plaza sights and sounds and smells were soothing to his senses. He stood patiently, calming himself, and in that brief lingering heard the man and woman coming from the east. The man was speaking roughly, the woman's reply was firm. They entered the cone of diffused light spread from the hotel windows, saw him, and had no choice. They must speak.

McGregor wrestled mightily with himself that afternoon, and came forth with a decision. He had belittled Aberdeen's fear but he was no longer confident in his own plan. The "ifs" crept into his mind and unnerved him. What if Jaramillo was discovered? What if Aberdeen lost his nerve and made a foolish break? What if he was left high and dry with, say, no more than two or three days to clear out safely? He had to prepare another exit.

So, doodling, adding up the pros and cons, McGregor faced the truth, not only his situation but his wife's. He was deluding himself these days in thinking she still cared; and considering his future, with or without her, made it an easy decision. McGregor slipped into a fine bout of self-pity: after all he had given her, a good house and plenty of everything, she did not give a continental damn. Not only that, she had become a cold fish, she deserved no second chance, not the way he intended to live. Let her visit that dried-up sister in Albuquerque. He'd promise to come down in a few weeks and talk it all over . . . but she'd wait fifty years for that little talk.

McGregor was so much taken with his bright dream of the future that he dawdled half an hour thinking of well-shaped, blond-haired women who appreciated a real man . . . and did he have a sure-fire emergency exit? Thank God, he had one made-to-order. It simply could not miss; it was foolproof. Why? Because he would use his wife. On that cheerful note, McGregor locked his office and went home.

He was unnaturally polite at supper. He ate with a minimum of his inbred bad manners and lingered over his coffee in well-planned malice. He had not intended broaching the subject of his selling out for at least two weeks, but that point was the keynote of his plan. He edged toward it cautiously, coming by way of Jones's as it were.

"A nice night."

"Yes, Bruce."

"Did you get out today?"

"I cleaned the house."

"You need fresh air," McGregor said. "Let's walk down and see the sights."

"Very well, Bruce."

McGregor helped carry the dishes to the kitchen and waited on the front porch until she came with a light shawl over her shoulders. He opened the gate and guided her along the empty road beneath the cottonwood trees in the murmurous night. He spoke of the trials and business and said obliquely, "Judith, have you changed your mind?"

"No, Bruce."

"I've been thinking," McGregor said heavily. "You're right and I'm wrong. You need a visit. A man can get by in this one-horse town, but for a woman like you—"

Unknowingly, almost in innocence, McGregor triggered her into pent-up reply.

AMBUSCADE

"Like me," she said. "What do you know of a woman like me, Bruce?"

"Know?" McGregor said. "You're my wife."

"Am I?" Judith McGregor said. "I have been thinking, too, and I was not entirely honest with you."

Now he must play it to the hilt. He said roughly, "Another man?"

"No, but when I said I would visit my sister, I did not make it clear that I was not coming back—"

"Yes, you did," McGregor said, "and I don't blame you. I'm going to sell out . . . don't argue with me, I made up my mind. I'll come down later and we'll have a good talk, eh?"

"—to you," she finished. "It makes no difference if you stay or go. I am through."

This was more than he hoped for, if he could swallow his singed pride . . . but he would swallow anything to be safe. As they came off Pueblo Road into the south plaza he raised his voice.

"Oh, you are! Well, you listen to me. I won't stand for any monkey business!"

"Bruce," she said. "It's no use."

"Hell's fire!" McGregor said loudly. "I've been forgetful, I admit it. Like that ditch and Cisneros—"

He looked up and saw Norcross before the Bar B office. It was the wry humor of fate that he shouted his latest irritation and saw the cause in the same moment; and even as he played the role he could not erase the suspicion that maybe, just maybe, there was more here than met the eye. But the opportunity was heaven-sent. McGregor did not waste a moment.

"Evening, John," he said, and stopped, forcing Judith to face the man.

"Mac," Norcross said. "Ma'am."

"Good evening," Judith McGregor murmured.

95

"Busy night," McGregor added heartily.

"A lot of commotion," Norcross said. "A lot of business."

"Yes," McGregor said, and put a knife-edge on his voice. "Everybody lets off steam these days . . . and nights!"

"Natural thing to do, Mac."

"Oh, come off it," McGregor said. "I call it lucky we just happened to be talking about Mister Norcross . . . in a left-handed way . . . and here he is."

"Ma'am," Norcross said, "has he been drinking hundred proof?"

"Not a whiff," McGregor said, "but I am about to make up for lost time." He turned to his wife with elaborate courtesy. "Mister Norcross is mighty handy around a house. Why don't you ask him to walk you home while I go find a bottle?"

Norcross stood fast. He had no time for foolish quarrels tonight. But McGregor was gone, striding rapidly toward the saloon, before she could protest. He faced her in angry embarrassment, and Judith McGregor bent her head.

"I am sorry—"

"He's drunk," Norcross said.

"No . . . please don't be angry with him."

"I'm not," Norcross said, "but he's right. You can't go home alone. Want me to get him?"

"Please don't," she said. "I can manage."

"Here," he said gruffly. "None of that!"

He took her arm and walked her from the plaza into the comforting gloom of Pueblo Road; and she did not speak until he opened her gate. There, thank the night, her face was masked by darkness. She could hide part of her shame. But Norcross had heard enough—too much, in fact—to be polite.

"This is a hard town on a woman," he said.

"Please," she said. "It does not concern you . . . and I thank you for walking me home."

"Wait," he said. "Just what did you want me to say?"

"Nothing, not a word."

Hat in hand but never meek, for he had his fill of meekness watching her, Norcross spoke his mind.

"Not a word?" he said. "You know I heard too much. You keep apologizing for him and that burns me. I'll tell you what I think of your husband. Somebody ought to one of these days—"

"No—"

"You're too good for him!"

"Please . . . please?"

"And the sooner you boot him out," Norcross said coldly, "the better off you'll be. That's the honest truth."

He turned but she stopped him, the first time she had touched him.

"Why do you say that?"

"Because I know you."

"How can you?" she said.

"Because I do," Norcross said. "Want to know what I thought when he brought you up here five years ago? I labeled you a damn fool, and McGregor was worse. Understand, I'd say it to his face. Tell him if you want. But you and McGregor! Like a mare and bull in harness, excuse me for saying it, but it's the truth—"

"Please—!"

"Stop excusing yourself," Norcross said. "Stand up on your hind legs and do a little yelling. My God, woman, I know the man. I've never been inside your house but I can tell you he's got it stuffed with all the junk that matters to him . . . not you, but him. I'll bet there's a couple dust-catching rugs and some of those cockeyed tables and chairs, and that bric-a-brac—

hell, reminds me of a funeral parlor. And where do you rate? Why, he stuck you up there on the wall like a tintype. You, of all people, with these flowers and that garden out back and the way you'd like to live here. If I—" He caught himself in time and stepped back through the gate. "Good night, ma'am."

───────── Eight ─────────

ENTERING THE SALOON AT TEN-THIRTY, NORCROSS SAW McGregor drinking whiskey at the bar and choked the impulse to boot him outside. He made his way through the crowd to the big table where Jess Dobernik waved like a man seeing salvation.

"Hey, John. They're skinning me alive. Want this seat?"

"I'll give it a whirl," Norcross said. "Two stacks, please."

Jaramillo's thick brows lifted and the other players stiffened as Norcross took the chair. A man rarely bought in with two stacks; it meant lack of confidence or, knowing Norcross, that he intended to bull the game. A ripple pulsated outward as the cards were dealt. Words passed along: Norcross is out for blood . . . gather round, pilgrims . . . now watch old Sal.

Men shoved and squirmed into position, heads vaporish in smoky shadow above the circular lamp shade, watching the eight heads and sixteen hands and the cards all displayed in the merciless light, outlined starkly against the green cloth. They waited expectantly and were not disappointed. Norcross made his weight felt in the third hand. He stayed, drew three cards, and bet the ten-dollar limit. No one called, the cards were passed, and Jaramillo cupped the chip rack in his big hands, face expressionless as he prepared to meet that challenge.

He was the dealer. He ran the game and, as such, must meet all challenges . . . and more, being a professional, must win. Not necessarily money, but he dared not allow a player to dominate him. There were subtle ways of beating a man down in a poker game. A good dealer's first move, when the action quickened, was inevitable. The crowd waited two rounds before Jaramillo, leaning back, caught the saloon-keeper's nod of assent.

"Gentlemen," he said. "What's your pleasure?"

"I smell smoke," one player answered.

"Smoke don't cook," Jaramillo said. "Do you want fire? It's your choice, gentlemen. Do we take off the lid?"

He was in his element, his face glistening with sweat and lamp reflection, the cigar drooping from the corner of his thick mouth. He heard the appreciative hum, the soft, nervous laughter as he dropped the challenge. Norcross looked up and nodded.

"Got to be a hundred percent," Jaramillo said. "House rule. Joe, Arturo . . . Cory?"

"Fine by me," Aberdeen said. "Long as I last."

"Table stakes?" Jaramillo asked then.

"No . . . yes . . . no."

"Let's get it straight," Jaramillo said patiently. "The house will try to meet all bets. You can play table stakes and back up, but name your amount."

One by one, each man announced for table stakes and thumped his wallet on the table, signifying he was backing up with every cent in his possession. Six men announced sums varying from two hundred to six hundred dollars. Norcross made no move.

"Well, John?" Jaramillo asked.

Norcross dropped a crumpled wad of bills beside his chips.

"That," he said. "And this."

He reached inside his coat and withdrew a leather bag. He fingered the drawstring and spilled part of the contents on the table. The twenty-dollar gold pieces gleamed in the lamplight. Norcross waited a moment, scooped them back into the bag, and returned it to his inside coat pocket.

"I'll play these back," he said. "One thousand, all double eagles . . . deal!"

Escudero moved along the bar until he found a better view of the table. He saw the shining reflection of the gold pieces, only a flashing, miserly look before shifting bodies cut off the sight, but that was enough. He padded back to his corner stool and hunched contentedly over his beer. Jess Dobernik paused beside him and winked.

"You see it?"

"*Si.*"

"That got him," Dobernik said. "Right in the gut."

"I know," Escudero said happily.

"Watch him," Dobernik said. "I'll pass the news."

"Remember," Escudero said. "He's for me!"

Jaramillo opened a fresh deck and shuffled the cards. He dealt and play resumed; but now he tried to analyze Norcross's behavior—angry at himself tonight, at the world, one drink too many, or what? But double eagles, one thousand dollars' worth! Exactly the sum in gold meant for Poppa Montoya. Jaramillo was suddenly concerned for Cory Aberdeen; but Cory, engrossed in the rare thrill of an open game, had missed the inference of the gold pieces. Insensitivity was bliss at times.

"Discards," Jaramillo said. "Your deal, Nate."

He played on, cleverly avoiding head-on tangles with

Norcross, letting the others increase the bets and set the rising tempo.

"Cards . . . two to you . . . and three there . . . the bet is here . . . this hand raises ten."

What a pack of blind baboons watching the game, breathing down his neck like bull-windy horses, pop-eyed over the fate of a few homeless dollars. If they only knew!

"The straight wins."

Very well, he would show them how Jaramillo met a challenge and played with the lid off, him alone, facing more than just another man. Let them crowd around, he'd give them a free lesson in poker tonight. . . . But he knew, as he watched Norcross, that it was not poker. This was one man against another. One man would break tonight. Jaramillo had never broken.

"The queens win . . . your deal, Jim."

Slowly the hours passed, the play grew higher, the table emptied. The first man dropped at midnight, the second broke at twelve-thirty. Aberdeen cashed in at one o'clock. At two-thirty, four men played; at three, Jaramillo faced Norcross across the ash-encrusted table.

"Just the two of us," he said. "Quit or play?"

"I'll try a few," Norcross said.

"Strip deck?"

"No."

Jaramillo smiled. "Hard to get openers, John."

"Any pair opens," Norcross said.

That tore off the roof. Two men bucking heads was certain to bring violent action, but playing a wide-open game was sudden death. A man had all the latitude in the world. He could bluff on any hand . . . oh yes, the children had departed, only the men remained.

"Any pair," Jaramillo agreed. "My deal."

Now it was a tight, personal matter beneath the garish light. Norcross won a hand, Jaramillo won three in a row, all small plays which meant nothing. They were jockeying, playing out the little hands, the window dressing; for it was only a matter of time before the big hand was dealt and the finish came.

At three-fifteen, with Jaramillo dealing, Norcross read his cards and opened for fifty dollars. Jaramillo studied his hand, called, and raised a hundred. It had come at last!

"And a hundred," Norcross said.

"And a hundred."

"Again."

Jaramillo held three tens. The feeling had never been stronger in his heart.

"Call," he said, "and raise two more."

"And two more."

"Call," Jaramillo said.

He had chosen his time to stop raising, show a tiny sign of weakness, drag the red herring before he heard the draw.

"Cards?"

"Two."

Jaramillo dealt and watched Norcross slide those cards beneath the three held . . . and never look. Jaramillo laid the deck aside and heard the hiss of breath above him.

"Play these," he said. "Your bet."

Well, he thought, what did you hold, Norcross? Three of a kind, or a pair with a kicker? The odds against Norcross making fours or filling were astronomical. And Norcross had not looked. That was a good play in some games, against some men, but not Sal Jaramillo . . . not against him! So here was the man who came to break him, put the fear of God in his heart.

"Your bet," Jaramillo repeated softly. "The grandstand don't work with me, John. You know that. Better look at your draw."

Norcross reached slowly into his coat pocket. He opened the leather sack and turned it over. The double eagles spilled across the table, glinting wickedly in the light.

"One thousand," Norcross said.

Deep inside Jaramillo something quivered, one drop of water falling from an inviolable snowcap; it elongated, fell, and betrayed him. It was not the money or the bluff. For in that moment Norcross looked up and met Jaramillo's eyes; and Jaramillo saw the executioner. Norcross knew, beyond doubt, and this was the moment.

"Well, gambler," Norcross said. "The bet is made."

Jaramillo had never looked away from another man's eyes across a poker table; to do so was to begin the private tragedy that would haunt him forever, the start of an emptiness that ruined a man. All the games in the world had nothing to do with this bet or the man's face across the table. One moment Jaramillo was tensing his hand to push the chips forward . . . the next he tossed his hand away and smiled.

"You win," he said. "The game is closed."

He sized Norcross's chips and paid off, his hands rock-steady on the cloth. Then, as he pushed back and rose, Norcross opened both hands and lifted his cards. No one had moved, everyone was truly breathless now, for a man never showed his hand after running a whizzer.

Norcross turned the cards and spread them faceup on the cloth for all to see—a pair of deuces and three unmatched, useless cards. That was the final touch, adding humility to defeat.

Jaramillo said, "Stand aside," and walked from the table, but the first nervous titter exploded and the laughter chased him from the saloon, the laughter that marked his finish in Rio Arriba. Norcross had ruined him here, the story would run downriver faster than water, until

everyone knew how Jaramillo was bluffed and broken
. . . and what did it matter? Not a bit.

Sal Jaramillo walked steadily, head up, through the
hotel lobby to the stairs and down the dark hall to his
room. He locked the door and faced the window, willing
his thoughts from the sound of laughter, thinking only of
himself and what he must do.

Nine

NORCROSS GAVE ONE ORDER TO THE BARTENDER. "DRINKS on me," and walked a gauntlet of backslaps and fulsome praise into the night.

"Here, Juan."

The need for secrecy had ended. They waited for him in the plaza, the men who wore well with time and extended no foolish praise. Norcross joined them under the trees where night wind sliced through the limp wetness of his shirt and chilled his back.

"He go upstairs?"

"Yes," Felipe said, "and everyone is ready."

"So he knows?" Mundo asked.

"He knows," Norcross said, "but he won't try tonight. He'll need a horse and he does not own one. Felipe, you and Mundo have a new job starting tomorrow. Watch the livery barn and corrals. He might try there."

"That is true," Mundo said. "I think we better take a look tonight, eh?"

"If you wish," he said.

"Come, Felipe," Mundo said. "We will tell Escudero as we go."

The sheriff gestured upward toward the darkened hotel windows.

"What is he thinking now, Juan?"

"Same as us," Norcross said. "Wondering how we did it, who it was. But he won't worry long over spilled milk. He'll make up his mind, and then he'll move."

"How long do you give him?" the sheriff asked.

"Two days at most."

"And the others . . . will he tell them now?"

"He'll pass the word," Norcross said. "We'll get them all. I'm going to bed, Eloy. Get yourself some sleep."

McGregor had downed a few drinks to create an impression, but thereafter dumped his whiskey and kept his head. He left the saloon when Norcross entered and ambled homeward, smiling at the stars. He stumbled over the threshold, banged clumsily into furniture while he raided the pantry, impersonated a half-drunk, unhappy man. When he opened the bedroom door she rose up and spoke one word.

"No!"

"Excuse me, madam," McGregor said thickly. "Wrong room."

He retired to the parlor and stretched out on the sofa. Tomorrow morning, instead of repentance, he would pursue his advantage and make it possible to put her on a stage at any time. That was the important factor—get her mad and keep her so mad she'd pack her bags and leave on five minutes' notice. Dozing off, McGregor thought of her and Norcross. The idea tickled him in a bitter way. Maybe she'd end up with that runt and have a litter of midgets.

Jaramillo had one final test. He went downstairs and found, as expected, a pseudosleeping man beside the back door. Crossing the yard to the outhouse, he heard faint sound in the stable. He remained a reasonable time before returning to his room . . . the last doubt was gone. He lit the lamp and followed his usual routine, undressing, having a drink, washing, hanging his clothes neatly in the closet. Ten minutes later he sat in darkness. Wind flapped the shade, the last tired sounds drifted upward from the plaza.

How had Norcross found him out?

Jaramillo journeyed backward into spent time, searching out his error. It was not a difficult task. He came quickly and logically to the human element—Curly and Lovato. Jaramillo wasted no breath cursing their mortal souls. It was done, he must look to himself. Cradling the brandy bottle between his knees, lighting a cigar, he tried to place himself in Norcross's mind. What else did Norcross know?

Well, it followed inevitably that Norcross knew he was not alone. And just as surely, Norcross did not know those names. Aberdeen and McGregor were still safe . . . but for how long?

Jaramillo could not estimate the number of Bar B men in town. Numbers were unimportant. Placement was paramount—where were they, how had Norcross stationed them to anticipate his final move? Norcross was playing with him like a cat cuffing a mouse, giving him freedom to run blindly into the noose. And why? Because he had to make the try . . . and take his share of the money with him.

Jaramillo laughed soundlessly. How he had warned Cory and Mac about the money! Be careful, don't panic, don't rush, if the money was found on them, that was curtains. Oh yes, and what could he do now?

Norcross was waiting patiently, knowing exactly what he was thinking up here in the dark. Norcross wanted him to take the money, not for additional evidence but, as honey on sweet rolls, for the added satisfaction when they shot him down or dragged him to the rope.

Well, he would not disappoint them. He would take the

money and make his run. There was still a chance. No matter tonight, he was the best gambler in the river country. No matter the odds, he'd find the hole.

So . . . how did they expect him to plan and act? What time of day or night, out what window or down what stair or through what roof? Oh, no, nothing complicated. Keep it simple and direct. Even now, Norcross was predicting his next move: he must warn the others. And why must he warn them? Because Norcross knew him so well. He had his code and a man lived by those stained ethics, no matter the cost. But warning Cory and Mac was much more than being faithful—if he could manage it, he not only kept faith with himself but improved his own chance. For Cory and Mac might panic and draw off a few hounds.

He must have a horse . . . and where did a man get horses?

Jaramillo sat unmoving until gray dawn streaked the room. At six o'clock, the bottle empty, his plan was made. He lay back and slept within the minute, untroubled by clinging doubts.

Ten

WALKING INTO TOWN THAT MORNING, TWO INDIANS SAW the men guarding the north road. They met a compatriot just returned from Ranchos and exchanged confidences.

"What is this?" one said. "You see these men?"

"Yes," the second said. "Is it that way south, Hernando?"

"Sure," Hernando said. "And look at them here in the plaza."

"Are the Comanches coming again?" the first said. "To have so many watchdogs. Maybe we better warn the pueblo."

"Ho," the second said. "Get the kids inside, pull up the ladders."

"And your old woman."

"Speak for yourself, man. Let the Comanches have her."

They spoke their own tongue, faces graven beneath their blanket cowls, jostled by people who heard their guttural speech and knew it must be very serious, for Indians had no sense of humor.

"I'll tell you," the first said. "Instead of getting drunk, I'm going to watch."

"Who?"

"Him . . . there in his window. I know some of these men."

"Oh, Juan Norcross. Yes, I heard a little rumor last night. You think there might be trouble?"

"Listen," the first said. "If I thought he was after me, I would not stop at the pueblo. I would be passing Blue Lake at this moment. Let's get over in the shade. It's too hot here."

Norcross stood in his window, all the tension drained from his body. Felipe had come to report all clear, received the day's orders, and gone forth to place the men. Norcross saw them lounging in the plaza, waiting for Jaramillo to show himself. Others guarded the dining room, the lobby, all the roads. Jaramillo would not speak a single word to man or beast without their knowledge.

"Juan."

Old Escudero stood in the hall doorway, a veritable bag of bones. What a man, Escudero—sleep meant nothing to him.

"Yes, Cisco?" he said.

"Our pigeon sleeps yet?"

"Till noon," Norcross said. "Where will you be then?"

"No matter," Escudero said. "But with your permission, I will move freely tonight."

"Anything you wish," Norcross said. "So you have my feeling—he will try it tonight?"

"I have that feeling, Juan."

"And come your way?"

Escudero smiled. "I have hopes."

"Good hunting, Cisco," he said. "But alive . . . I want that order obeyed."

"*Si*," Escudero said. "Alive, Juan. But he may be scratched up a little, eh?"

"Within limits," Norcross said sternly, and then he

111

laughed, and the old man entered the room and patted his shoulder.

"I understand," Escudero said gently. "When I think of Roberto, I want to do terrible things to this man. But I know that is wrong because we must obey the law and show we are not savages, not as bad as him, eh? But it is hard, Juan, very hard. Just think—one snap of the rope and he'll be dead. No penance! Aiih, that is why I must tickle him a little before we give him to the sheriff." Escudero sighed regretfully. "To think I have changed so, become reasonable. I have turned into a milkmaid."

"You?" Norcross said. "I would see the cows you milk!"

Jaramillo woke at twelve o'clock and spent time lavishly, shaving, taking a cold-water bath, putting on fresh socks and underwear.

"Hah," he told the face in the mirror. "You'll win no beauty prize."

He laid out his clean brown suit coat, picked the lining thread loose with a needle, and folded the lining back. Opening the corner cache, he spread the money on the bed, pushing the gold pieces aside. Holding the needle delicately, he sewed thin packets of money securely against the thick coat cloth, replaced the lining, and sewed it to each sheaf of bills. Finally, rethreading, squinting one eye like a seamstress, he resewed the seam, bit the thread, and knotted the end. Not for secrecy . . . who cared about that? . . . but he would move like the wind tonight and nothing must constrict his body.

"Well now," he said. "And what of you, eh?"

He jiggled the handful of gold pieces, slipped one into his pants watch pocket, and poured the others back in the hole. He replaced the boards, snugged the bed against the wall, and turned to other imperative tasks.

He cleaned his .38, put on shirt and trousers, and slipped the holster over his waist belt against his right hip pocket. Shrugging into the coat, he distributed eighteen cartridges in the two large pockets; and then he broke the habit of years. He shoved loose money into one pocket, six cigars in another. All the other pieces and parts of his life went into the battered grip and under the bed. He was traveling light. He stood at the window a minute, studying the scene below, picking the loafers who did not belong.

"Nine—no, ten," he counted. "And more . . . long odds."

Going downstairs, he spoke to the day clerk, to six other men between lobby and dining room. He joked with the waitress and traded banalities with a fat drummer he had known for several years. He ate slowly, lit a cigar, and stepped outside.

"Now," he murmured. "Follow me, Norcross."

He turned left, not right, and toured the plaza. He visited the general store, the hardware, the drugstore, the saloons, he spoke with twenty-odd people before he went slowly down the road toward the livery barn; and even then he added another touch.

The children were playing under the cottonwood tree across from the barn. Jaramillo squatted down and watched them play a mysterious game with sticks and cabalistic marks in the dust. He joked with the boys, patted the lone tomboy's shiny black crown, and gave them all a nickel.

"*Adios,* my friends," he smiled.

Then he crossed the road into the barn and greeted the helpers.

"Got that gentle horse?"

"Out back, Sal."

"*Bueno,*" Jaramillo said, and approached the corral where Aberdeen worked a horse beside the fence.

"Cory," Jaramillo said cheerfully. "Cigar?"

"Thanks . . . want the sorrel?"

"Yes."

He leaned on the fence until Aberdeen led the sorrel

from the barn. Taking the reins, head masked by the horse, Jaramillo spoke softly.

"They're onto me."

"SAL—!"

"Stand fast," Jaramillo said. "Fiddle with that cinch . . . listen to me. I'm leaving tonight. I want your best horse, that grulla. Saddled, small sack of grub, Winchester in the boot. At one o'clock tonight, tie him south of the road, just east of Carson's house."

"Sal," Aberdeen said. "Do they know—?"

"Steady!"

Jaramillo mounted the sorrel, rubbed his hips into the saddle, and grinned easily at Aberdeen.

"They don't know and I won't talk. You're on your own, Cory. Don't bolt and you'll make out."

He lifted one hand in casual farewell and trotted eastward, a big man taking his customary ride. He had dropped a silent thunderbolt in the quiet afternoon.

Cory Aberdeen did not trust his legs. He leaned against the corral fence and smoked the cigar to a nubbin while he faced up to the danger. He could depend on one solid fact—Sal would never betray him. But wait another month? Could he stand a week, even a day! Aberdeen walked through the barn and stepped next door into McGregor's office.

"Mac."

McGregor looked up with a wry smile. "Lose your shirt last night?"

"Won fifty," Aberdeen said woodenly.

"I just heard it turned into a stem-winder," McGregor said. "That sort of game is too rich for your blood. . . . What's the matter, Cory?"

"Oh, nothing much," Aberdeen said thinly. "Sal just got a horse . . . they're onto him!"

McGregor laid his pencil aside and closed the ledger.

He leaned back in his swivel chair, his round face losing its ruddy color.

"He's sure?"

"Yes, he's sure," Aberdeen said.

"What did he say?" McGregor asked. "Try to repeat it exactly, Cory."

"He's making his run tonight," Aberdeen said. "I'm to tie a good horse east of Carson's at one o'clock."

"Will you?"

"Yes," Aberdeen said. "For nobody but him."

"What else?"

"For us not to worry," Aberdeen said. "He won't talk if—"

"Get a grip on yourself," McGregor said. "Sal is right. Don't bolt."

"Who the hell is running?" Aberdeen said. "I'd trust Sal with my life."

"You are," McGregor said, "and I'm damn glad to see you using common sense. . . . I wonder, was it Jones or Lovato?"

"Mac," Aberdeen said, "it makes no never mind who it was or what happened. I want to know how long you'll stick?"

"Why, as planned," McGregor said calmly. "If I was a praying man, I'd say some words for Sal tonight. But like he said, we're on our own. Me, I'm sitting pat."

"Me too," Aberdeen said fervently.

They stared at each other for the last time, two conspirators unraveling at invisible seams, bolstering each other with glib tongues while their hearts beat like frightened rabbits. Aberdeen mustered a lame grin, "See you tomorrow," and went from the office to face the endless passage of time.

McGregor slumped deeper into the chair and propped his boots on the desk. He had anticipated this moment;

now it had come, he dared not hesitate. He trusted Jaramillo, but Cory was another matter. Cory might break and run at any moment; and caught . . . dear Lord, he could hear Cory babbling now. Oh, Cory would stake out the horse tonight. He had that breed of courage; but once he made that final gesture and sneaked back to the barn, anything could happen.

McGregor made his decision in that moment. He came from the chair, closed the desk, and put on his hat.

"My dear wife," he whispered. "I hope your sister has her spare bedroom ready."

Rio Arriba enjoyed a spirited court session that afternoon. A young man was on trial for rape, unusual to say the least in such a compliant country, and several spectators nursed more than idle interest in the outcome. Judge Webster presided, instructed the jury, and pondered the question during the wait: was the young woman guilty of resistance or the young man guilty of misplaced confidence? The jury returned with a verdict, Webster rendered his sentence, and the session was closed. Leading Runnells into his chambers, he shucked the sweaty robe and smiled.

"Well, did she or did she not?"

"To be honest," Runnells said, "I was thinking of tonight."

"To be forthright with you," Webster said, "I have never been so impatient with time."

"Heard anything from John?"

"Nothing," Webster said. "You saw him at dinner."

"Yes, and heard him," Runnells said. "He smiled twice and told a joke. What does that mean? You know him the best.

"Well," Webster said mildly, "I remember a time eight years ago—or was it nine? No matter, and no need for details. He was having trouble with a bunch of big boys and it was due for the showdown that night. Mind you, he was alone in this particular fracas. A personal affair. We ate supper together, most enjoyable meal with him in years. He smiled and joked and talked about everything under the sun.''

"He was scared?"

"No, George," Webster said. "Not the way you mean. Afraid, yes, but not for himself. Afraid for others, afraid of how his action would affect others. That stage where a man is sure and yet uncertain, the way a man feels once in his life . . . with luck. As I was saying, he settled the argument that night. Oh, don't let his size fool you, George. He used a chair leg. There were only six of them, so it was fair enough, and not bad odds . . . for him. Of course, it wasn't deadly serious. What I am getting at is, I noted a certain incisiveness in him this noon.''

"Tonight then?"

"I would take odds on it."

"But how can he know?" Runnells asked.

"He knows," Webster said. "Don't ask me how or why—he just knows. It's a feeling."

"You know how I feel?" Runnells asked.

"Partly . . . but get it off your chest."

"Like the executioner," Runnells said.

"No, George," Webster said. "Norcross is the executioner. Come along, I'm bone-dry. . . . By the way, have you known many executioners?"

"No."

"I have," Webster said. "And they all share one mutual feeling . . . they detest their job."

------------------ Eleven ------------------

THE LIGHTS CAME ON, NEVER SO BRIGHT AS THE STARS
in the high blue sky, but bright enough for men to live
and die by. Small boys played tag among the wagons; for
them the lights were never too bright. To the old men on
the plaza benches, watching youth run and shout, the
lights were dim. No matter the time of day, someone was
forever closing the circle of dark and light. The rhythm
was endlessly repeated. The young cried impatiently,
"How can the hours last so long?" and the old felt the
heavy beat of the clock. What came tonight, tomorrow,
next week and next year? Everyone was conscious of
time.

"He comes," an old man said.

"Make yourself small," his neighbor whispered.
"Whatever it is, we must see it."

"How can you be sure?"

"I feel it," the old man said. "And look, the Indians
wait. They are never wrong."

They watched John Norcross step from the dining room
and walk beneath the portal, a squat shape in the night;
and he, in turn, saw the wagons, buggies, and horses,
the old men sitting patiently, the Indians forming indef-

118

inite lumps against the walls. Felipe joined him and he said, "Come along," and crossed the plaza to Pueblo Road where Bar B men waited with horses. "He has started the poker game," Norcross told them. "I am going for a ride." He mounted his black horse and reined north, riding because he could not sit or stand or idle through these meaningless early hours. He reached the junction and spoke to the men guarding both roads. He went half a mile toward the pueblo before turning back; and passing McGregor's he saw the lampshine in the windows and thought of her. . . .

As Norcross saw her face and passed on, McGregor heard the horse and glanced at the window which reflected the same lampshine in their eyes. He had come home early and talked late, and now he was over the first hurdle.

"Very well," he said. "Tomorrow then?"

"Yes."

"I'll buy your ticket now."

"Thank you," Judith said.

"Stage leaves at seven," McGregor said. "You catch the afternoon train at the junction. How many bags will you take?"

"Two," she said. "You can send whatever is left."

"I regret this," McGregor said, "but I won't argue. I won't ask you to wait any longer. Sometimes it's best for all concerned."

"I'm sure it is," she said. "When will you be home?"

"Don't worry," McGregor said. "I'm not in a drinking mood tonight . . . and I won't wake you up. I know my place."

He slammed on his hat and went from the house, riling the dust scarcely settled behind Norcross's horse. As McGregor approached the plaza, already dreaming of freedom, Norcross tied his horse outside the Bar B office. He brought a chair from the hall, placed it against the wall, and tilted back with his heels on the rung. He heard a scraping and saw Judge Webster coming from the lobby with another chair.

"Mind company, John?"

"Need it," Norcross said. "Cigar?"

"Thank you."

"One thing," Norcross said, holding the match. "When it starts, duck inside."

"Now, John—"

"Get inside," Norcross said flatly. "I'll bring them before you, Judge. You hang them!"

"Agreed. . . . My, but people are staying out late tonight."

Norcross saw his own men, the old men, the children, sensed movement and heard sound . . . saw McGregor enter the hotel, walking straight and sober. "Slowpoke!" A small boy taunted another. "Here I am!" The boys were flitting ghosts, painted in light, hidden by night, between the wagons and under the buggies. The old men sat unmoving and the Indians had not begun their long walk home.

"What's the time?" Norcross asked.

"Five after nine."

"Judge," Norcross said abruptly, "how old were you when you got married?"

"Eh . . . oh, thirty-two."

"Were you sure?"

Webster swung around and stared over his cigar. "Of course I was, and so was Corrie. What kind of leading question is that? You've known Corrie sixteen years. Do you think we're about to stage a knock-down-drag-out and split up the dishes?"

"No," he said. "But how did you know?"

"Lord love me," Webster laughed. "I didn't . . . it just happened. What are you trying to do, or prove? Just pass the time, or have you got a little *querida* tucked away that we don't know about?''

"Yes to the one," Norcross said. "No to the other."

"Which is which, boy?"

"Who cares," Norcross said. "Talk up a storm, Judge. Get me over the hump!''

·····Twelve·····

MANY MEN WERE CLIMBING A HUMP THAT NIGHT.

Jaramillo dealt the cards as if last night was forgotten. He ignored the reckless players who believed his strength was gone. They pecked at him, pushed their luck, took chances that led straight to bankruptcy. Having witnessed the bluffing of Jaramillo, they wanted a second-hand share of that glory tonight and every night he was fool enough to continue.

Jaramillo played his way through time. He saw McGregor enter the saloon and face the bar. McGregor turned, glass in hand, and met his gaze. McGregor looked into space, face indifferent, but lifted his glass in a silent toast. Jaramillo tugged his eyeshade in reply. McGregor swung away and spoke to a neighbor. Jaramillo played on.

"Your health," Jose Bernal said.

"And yours," McGregor said. "Still holding those sheep?"

"Yes."

What good fairy had brought them together tonight? Bernal lived far down Ranchitos, and Bernal wished to sell a small bunch of old rams and ewes. What greater fortune brought the sheriff beside them at the most opportune moment?

"Are you ready to sell?" McGregor asked.

"I am thinking on it."

"I'll tell you," McGregor said. "My wife's taking the morning stage to visit her sister. I'll ride down after that and make you a price, eh?"

"If you would be so kind."

"Good," McGregor said. "Look for me between eight and nine, eh."

He finished his drink and said, "Evening, Eloy," and went from the saloon into the night. He had achieved perfection—hitch up the buggy, saddle under the blanket, bring Judith to the stage, go on down Ranchitos toward Bernal's without suspicion. Beat the stage to Taos Junction, relieve Judith of her innocent burden, and it did not matter when Aberdeen was caught.

Escudero rode from the night and joined the Bar B group as McGregor passed, whistling merrily, giving them all a hearty greeting. Escudero lowered a large sack to the ground and poked the nearest man.

"Who is that?"

"Gordo, the fat commission man . . . what's that, Cisco?"

"Nothing."

"Nothing? Come on, let's see—"

"Stay there," Escudero said softly. "Kindly leave this sack alone."

The Bar B men grinned at the knife-edge in the old man's voice. Whatever it was, their respect was such that if Escudero had a bobcat or a pretty woman in the sack, they would stand clear. They waited in the night, smoking, talking softly, waiting for the big move.

* * *

Aberdeen sat in the barn office until his helpers called good night and his night man arrived. He strolled through the barn and stood beside the night man in the front doorway.

"Damn belly's acting up," he said. "Be back soon."

"You play tonight?"

"No," Aberdeen said. "Can't sit still."

He went up the road into the plaza and drank a bromo in the drugstore. He stopped by the saloon for one drink, complained about his stomach, and departed. Passing the Bar B office he paused and said, "What do you do for a bellyache?"

"Tried a bromo?" Norcross asked.

"Yes . . . didn't do nothing."

"Cut down on the chili," Webster laughed.

"Cut something," Aberdeen agreed querulously. "Giving me fits tonight."

He returned to the livery barn and sat glumly with the night man. "No use," he said. "Can't sleep."

"No better, eh?"

"Worse," Aberdeen said. "Might as well stay up. . . . Take the night off, Pepe. I'll handle things."

"If I can help—?"

"I'm no fit company," Aberdeen said. "Go on, see that girl in Prado."

"*Gracias*, Cory. I hope you feel better."

The night man escaped before Aberdeen could change his mind, for the boss was notoriously fickle in such moments. But he was in no danger. Alone, Cory Aberdeen prepared for the night.

He carried gear and his extra Winchester to the rear stall. He went to his living quarters behind the office, sacked up groceries and placed that sack beside the gear. He examined the grulla with minute care and gave the big horse a last feed of grain. Again in his room, he changed to moccasins, emptied his pockets of loose articles, and began a second set of preparations.

He opened the secret cubby in the ceiling and shoved the money pouch—including the gold pieces—into his saddlebag. He packed a few clothes, another sack of groceries, and stacked all beneath his bed. Then he returned to the bench in front and settled down to fight the hours.

At twelve-thirty Jess Dobernik stepped from the saloon and came along the boardwalk.

"Slow game," he reported. "Only five left."

"How long do you give them?"

"Any time now."

"Pass the word," Norcross said, and turned to Judge Webster. "Better get inside—" He pointed to the window. "There's George, come in the back way. Keep him company."

Webster made no protest but opened the door and joined Runnells at the office window.

"How can he stand it?" Runnells asked. "Out there cool as ice."

"Don't touch him," Webster said drily. "You'll suffer third-degree burns."

Waiting was a tedious business, almost disgusting when they considered what could happen on the plaza. Nor were the smells behind the livery barn comparable to roses. Midnight wore away and Mundo Molimo stifled a grunt of anger. Then Felipe leaned forward, sniffed like a hound, and touched Mundo's arm.

"There!"

They saw a man lead a horse from the barn and trot northward around the curve of the slope toward the canyon road. Following, they watched him tie the horse under a tree just east of Carson's house. Felipe put his mouth to Mundo's ear.

"Aberdeen?"

"Yes . . . I'll tell them."

"Hurry!"

Felipe trailed Cory Aberdeen back to the barn and waited beside the big corral. Mundo Molimo, pausing to examine the horse and remove the rifle from the saddle boot, ran swiftly to the plaza. He found Stash Dobernik and Escudero, and gave his precious information. As he turned away, Stash went for Norcross and Escudero gave a soft command to the eager men.

"When he comes, let him reach the horse!"

"But—"

"You hear me?" Escudero hissed.

He gathered his plump sack and rode the canyon road past Carson's house until he saw the tied horse under the tree. He prowled the southside ditch, moved twenty steps eastward, and opened the sack. He spread the contents in the ditch for a distance of some twenty yards. Then he mounted and stationed himself on the north side of the road, across from the tied horse. He shook out his rope and whispered fondly to the finest roping horse in the upper river country; and while he waited, Felipe spoke to Mundo Molimo.

"This door or the front, eh?"

"Yes."

"Which do you want?"

"You are the oldest," Mundo said.

"Ha, the back then . . . come, let's get the horses. This pigeon is ours."

"Aiih!" Mundo said. "Think of it—Aberdeen!"

"Wonderful, wonderful . . . but who is the third man?"

Stash Dobernik reached Norcross at the same moment his brother hurried from the saloon. Stash told the great news just received. Jess said, "Game broke up," and they waited for the command. Norcross seemed to grow before their eyes.

"Pass the word down the south road," he said. "Felipe and Mundo can't leave the barn."

"I'll go," Jess said, and was gone.

"John," Stash Dobernik said, "how will Jaramillo try it?"

"Upstairs," Norcross said. "Downstairs. Any time, from any place . . . just be ready."

He moved to the edge of the boardwalk and loosed the Colt in his holster. Aberdeen, he thought, Cory Aberdeen!

If there was another man, he would know by dawn. He had them now . . . there was no way out.

127

·············· Thirteen ··············

Many men had labored up a grade that night. All of them, in various ways, reached the hump at twenty minutes past one o'clock—the patient old men, the stoic Indians, the men who knew . . . all were rewarded in their separate ways.

Jaramillo bought drinks for the players and glanced at the Seth Thomas clock above the archway. The front lights were snuffed and he saw clearly through the windows into the plaza. He counted three wagons and a buggy at the rail, and the indistinct figures of men slipping into the plaza. They did not know how he would move, or when, from the lobby or his room, now or later. Call the bluff, always use the simple way.

"Well," he said, "good night, all!"

He walked slowly from the saloon and took in the plaza with one sweeping glance. He turned toward the lobby doors, fifteen short steps away, and pushed both hands up and behind his belt against his hips in a man's natural stretching motion after six hours in a chair. He walked, arching his back, and saw Norcross before the Bar B office. When Jaramillo came abreast the darkened dining room windows he drew the snub-nosed .38 in one smooth motion and leaped suddenly from the boardwalk between

128

two wagons. He saw Norcross leap, gun out, and then Jaramillo was racing toward the courthouse. At that point he veered eastward, scooped an old man off the nearest bench and carried him, like a ham in one arm. He heard the shouts and saw men closing, grouping before him.

"Would you kill an old man?" he called.

"Hold up!" Norcross shouted.

They faded back and Jaramillo burst through them to the road forks. He faked northward and swung east along the canyon road, dropped the old man, and ran for his life between the silent walls, past Carson's house, toward the downgrade where the road ran ribbon-white in the star-shine. He jumped the ditch, slipped the tie rope, and wheeled the grulla in a tight circle, fighting for and catching the stirrup, swinging upward with the grulla's momentum, digging in as he pointed for the road. He was one jump down the slope, the grulla gathering speed, great muscles coiling and springing, when he heard a whisper in the wind and felt the loop drop over his hat, his head, and catch his shoulders in a soft embrace. He fought the rope with one hand but that was a motion begun on the lean side of one second and ended on the fat side of the same second. By then he was jerked from the saddle, falling, striking earth on neck and shoulders, gun flying one way, hat another . . . and then Jaramillo screamed, for the rope horse had turned and he was in the ditch, the rope dragging him through liquid fire. He could not help himself. He screamed in pure agony and lost consciousness before they reached him and Norcross said, "Take him to the courthouse . . . now the barn!"

Cory Aberdeen meant to time his departure exactly. He sat his buckskin in the alleyway darkness, facing the front door, boots on his feet again, spurs poised for the first rake. No roads for him tonight. The moment he heard trouble on the plaza he was going through the front door,

across the road, into the night. Let them watch the roads.
They could not guard the limitless land. Once across the
road, heading west, an army could not take him. He leaned
forward, patted the fat curve of the saddlebag, and waited
unafraid. And then he heard the first shouts, a brief silence, and a sudden scream that chilled the night. Aberdeen hit the buckskin and came from the barn in a mad
rush. Someone shouted out back and he wanted to yell his
triumph as the buckskin cleared the road in two great
bounds; and before he could straighten in the saddle, see
the other horse and take preventive measures, that horse
came from the side and crashed the buckskin. Aberdeen
fought for his seat as the buckskin went up, lost its foot-
ing, and tumbled. Instinct made him kick loose and palm
the saddle, push himself away as the buckskin rolled; but
he was sailing and he struck the earth and rolled. He
clawed for his Colt but the holster was empty. Then it
seemed that two wildcats and a lion lit on his head. He
fought back, flailing both arms, kicking viciously. Someone said calmly, "Move your head, Mundo," and before
Aberdeen could move *his* head it received one hearty swipe
from a rifle barrel.

Norcross stood in the sheriff's office while around him,
in great waves of sound, voices echoed along the center
hall and multiplied in the plaza. How could so many people come from nowhere in a matter of minutes?

"How is he?" Norcross asked.

Jaramillo lay on his face, groaning between set teeth as
the doctor labored with pliers and tweezers. "Well, Doc?"

"He'll live . . . lay still, damn it!"

Cory Aberdeen was stretched behind the counter, the
right side of his face turning color from the rifle blow.
Chato Morales wet a towel and placed it on the swelling.

"Out of it?" Norcross asked.

"So-so," Chato grinned. "He'll live."

Norcross waited impatiently. In a moment they would know beyond any shadow of doubt. The sheriff finished ripping Jaramillo's coat apart, Runnells counted that money for the second time.

"Well?"

"Almost fifteen thousand, John."

"Eloy?"

The sheriff was thumbing the bills taken from Aberdeen's saddlebag. He licked his finger, counted the last sheaf, and turned.

"The same amount, Juan."

"No more?"

"Here," Escudero said. "From the gambler's pocket."

Norcross looked at the double eagle in Escudero's dirty palm. "One for the money," he said softly. "Two for the show . . . let him keep it! Shut that hall door, Stash!"

"Let me see," the sheriff said. "Five thousand from Jones. Fifteen thousand each from these two. Juan—!"

"One left," Norcross said. "It was a three-way split."

"But who—?" the sheriff asked.

"By tomorrow night," Norcross said, "some of you will entertain Aberdeen, eh? Everybody else back on the roads—I want more men between. Eloy, I want warrants."

"What kind, Juan?"

"Search," he said. "Signed, we'll fill them in if needed. We search every person leaving town."

The sheriff looked at Aberdeen and understood perfectly. Yes, they would find their third man. And then, like every man in the room, he watched Norcross. Juan could be excused if he wished to curse those two men, beat them, do as he wished. But how strange it was—Juan's face was smoothing out, he was becoming the man they knew and loved so well.

For it was true.

Norcross looked at Jaramillo, at Aberdeen, and felt the

old rage dying. He glanced at Escudero and let his face break into a smile. Jaramillo was a living pincushion, so punctured with cacti it would take a week to pluck him clean. Nothing had broken Jaramillo in the past, but tonight he was a broken man.

"Cisco," Norcross said, "you scratched him up a little."

"He will live," Escudero said mildly.

"Hah!" the sheriff said. "I doubt he will be able to climb the gallows steps."

"Oh yes," Escudero said. "I was very considerate. He needs only his neck and the soles of his feet for that. See, they are clean."

Fourteen

T HEY WAITED ON THE TALPA RIDGE THREE MILES SOUTH
of Rio Arriba. Norcross sat beside the road, dozing on his
arms, listening to the others debate the chance of catching
that last man. Men guarded every road this morning, even
between the roads, and the last man must run. Aberdeen
was entertaining unwelcome guests in the jail, persuasive
men who had carte blanche to inspire their fertile talents.
Aberdeen would warble like a lark within three hours.
That last, unknown man knew the truth as well as they.
He must run. In the meantime . . .

"Ho," Felipe called. "Here is Mundo."

Norcross rose and greeted Molimo; to the north, just
leaving town, a plume of dust marked the morning stage.

"Well?" he said.

"Three drummers," Mundo said. "A man from San
Luis, and the lady—"

"A woman!"

"Señora McGregor," Mundo said. "She—"

"I remember," the sheriff said. "I saw him last night.
She is going to visit her sister."

"Yes," Mundo said. "McGregor brought her to the
plaza in his buggy and went on toward Ranchitos."

"To Bernal's," the sheriff said. "To buy sheep."

133

"That's all?" Norcross asked.

"That is all, Juan."

Waiting for the stage, something went askew in Norcross's thoughts and refused to come unstuck.

"Do we search them all?" Felipe asked.

"Yes."

"But the lady—?"

"No exceptions," Norcross said. "Bag and baggage."

He wanted to turn away and leave the job to others; but it was his job. He had to face her one last time; for now, thinking back, he felt that she was leaving Rio Arriba for good. It was ungrounded thought; but the feeling was too strong in his heart.

He watched the stage grow in size, top the last rise, grind to a halt before the restraining line. The sheriff invited the passengers down while Chato climbed the stage and handed down all baggage from boot and rack. Judith McGregor stepped down, looked about in puzzlement, and saw Norcross.

"You understand?" he asked.

"Yes," she said. "But why—?"

"You know what happened last night," Norcross said. "We have no choice, ma'am. Which are your bags?"

"The Gladstone," she said. "That small black one."

"Come with me," Norcross said. "Chato, bring them."

He led her behind the stage where she could enjoy a measure of privacy. The sheriff and Chato ranged behind her and shut off the view of others. The drummers were protesting loudly, the man from San Luis was joking with Stash Dobernik. Not much doubt, he thought, they would draw a blank and make five enemies for life.

"I am sorry," Norcross said, "but we must be fair to all."

"I understand," she said. "Please don't wrinkle the—"

"Yes, ma'am," he said. "Here, Chato. I'll do it."

He unbuckled the Gladstone straps, smacked the lock, and laid back the halves of the big grip. He pushed a finger under the layers of tight-packed dresses and underthings, into one corner . . .

"Eh?" the sheriff said softly.

Norcross rubbed the slick surface of an oilskin pouch. He lifted the clothing and saw it tucked neatly in the corner. Then he knew it all as he pulled the string, exposed one green corner of the rolled money, and handed the pouch to the sheriff.

"What—?" she said thinly. "Oh, no . . . oh God!"

He had to face her, knowing at last what Webster meant—there was no logic, no reason, no time for the moment. A man simply knew and felt and was never the same. Norcross knew in that moment, and all the anger rose afresh within him. He wanted her, he must have her, and if ever a man had the chance to pave his own road to happiness, to make her a free woman, he was that man on this day. But he could not make an exception. He must take McGregor alive. And there was the bitter irony.

"I did not know," she whispered. "I was leaving . . . not coming back. . . . He—"

"I know," he said. "Can you ride?"

"Yes."

How little he knew about her, where she grew up, if she could ride, if she had been someone with shape and substance and mind before McGregor saw her in the white Harvey uniform. So much to discover, to learn, to feel, and no hope now. It was between them, plain at last in her eyes too, to see and feel, and it meant nothing.

"We are going to the Junction," he said. "You must return to town."

"I understand."

"Get a horse, Chato," he said. "Take her in, bring the others."

"*Bueno.*"

Norcross turned to the sheriff. "You see it?"

"Down Ranchitos," the sheriff said. "Then ride for the Junction—riding now—and catch the señora there."

"Chato," he said. "Hurry up."

They had a moment as Chato ran for horses and the sheriff went away to apologize to the other passengers.

"I'll tell you now," Norcross said. "I did not want it this way."

"It does not matter," she said.

"But it does," he said fiercely. "He used you . . . damn him, he used you!"

"It does not matter," she said. "Just give me time."

From the east rim of the river gorge they saw the faint dust of a rider gaining the west rim, a tiny figure brought larger by the glasses, a man on a black horse.

"Too fat," Felipe said. "We are gaining."

They descended into the depths, crossed the river, and attacked the west wall road. On the top, pushing hard, they raced for the Junction across the hardpan flats, into the skimpy timber that whiskered the low hills. Felipe ranged far ahead and waved them to the abandoned shed . . . the shed with its dusty, dry smell of horses gone many years, yet holding the undying whisper of what was once alive—and the manure where McGregor had rested his horse and broken that old spell of deathless life.

"Not far ahead," Felipe said.

They strung out the final mile through the timber, broke from the last forest bend into the cleared ground, saw the depot and a few cars on the switch track. Felipe shouted, "HO!"

McGregor was half a mile ahead, just entering the depot yard, slumped over his horse. Felipe's yell lifted him, he stared in utter disbelief. He spurred his horse across the tracks onto the road that wandered south toward Ojo Caliente beside the railroad grade. And then he jumped the

136

horse from road to right-of-way and leaped to the ground beside the section shack and pointed a gun at the crew lounging in the shade. He ran to their yellow handcar and pushed it down the track. He got the handles going up and down, and leaped aboard. He was a quarter mile down-track, building speed, when Norcross reached the crossing.

"How?" Felipe shouted. "It goes fast, eh?"

"The road," Norcross called. "Follow along."

"Our horses are tired—" Felipe nodded and led the way.

McGregor pumped desperately, spreading his feet wide on the swaying platform, hands slippery on the smooth handles. Too late to curse or think or wonder why. Just pump, build up speed, and think ahead. Their horses were dead beat and the road was longer than the track, and the track ran downhill all the way to Ojo Caliente. He had a chance. McGregor worked as he had never worked before; and slowly, gradually, he drew away. He saw them through the forest gaps as they raced along the bends and curls of the road, almost abreast, then dropping back, then out of sight. No thought for the money now, that was gone . . . the grade lifted invisible arms, drew with magnetic power, the little handcar sang and clattered over the rail joints. He was fairly flying, the handles moving so swiftly he could barely hold on, much less pump. McGregor straightened, wiped his face, glanced back . . . half a mile, by God, and gaining every yard. He turned as the handcar bit into a sharp, tight curve, wheels grinding against the rails. He was moving at least forty miles an hour . . . no, faster, the way the trees flashed by. He reached the apex of the curve and swooped around between the trees and saw the smoke ahead, then the stack, and looming before him, the black snout of the freight engine. . . .

* * *

137

Felipe climbed the bank and stood beside him in the tree shade. They looked down upon the engine, stopped now, black smoke rising lazily against the deep blue sky. The handcar was a twisted yellow toy in the grass, men were grouped about a smaller form covered by a coat.

"The engineer is shaking like a leaf," Felipe said. "He swears it was worse than hitting a cow."

"Dead?"

"Oh yes, Juan. A handle or the front of the engine. I do not know. No matter. . . . Now we can go home, eh?"

"Yes," Norcross said. "Now we can go home."

Fifteen

The wheel had come full turn. Judge Webster was on the bench. Pablo Lovato, restored to legal life, sat at the defense table. George Runnells waited for the first juryman, and in that climactic moment, hearing a small sound in the silence, saw an old man rise and face the judge.

"Yes?" Judge Webster said, as if expecting this interruption.

"Your Honor," the old man said politely, "that man has been tried and sentenced."

"He has?"

"Yes, Your Honor."

Judge Webster brought his gavel down smartly. "Case dismissed!"

George Runnells had grown many cubits in the past days; there remained a final ounce. He went forward and stared at Judge Webster in alarm.

"Sir, are you ill?"

"Never felt better, George."

"Then what—?"

"George," Judge Webster said, "Do you know of the Penitent Brothers, the Penitentes?"

"Yes, but—?"

"Pablo Lovato is a Brother," Judge Webster said. "The man he killed was a Brother. Did you hear that old man?"

"Yes—"

"He is the Hermano Mayor," Judge Webster said. "The Chief Brother here."

"But—"

"They tried Pablo Lovato," Judge Webster said, "And sentenced him. I can guess he must provide for the widow and child until she remarries or the child comes of age. That is his punishment."

"But—"

"How could you convict him?" Judge Webster said. "You cannot swear in a jury here without one or more Brothers in the box. . . . Now, do you see?"

George Runnells saw . . . at long last. What all of them, including Jaramillo, had known from the start—that Pablo Lovato had never been in danger from the law, could not be. George Runnells had been privileged to witness the greatest irony one man could perpetrate upon another. It was the measure of a man; it gave the true stature of John Norcross.

"I see," George Runnells said. "Dear God, I see it now . . . but the morals?"

"There are no morals involved," Judge Webster said quietly. "Only people."